# SHADOW HUNTER

## BOOK 1 OF ROSIE O'GRADY'S PARANORMAL BAR AND GRILL

## BR KINGSOLVER

**Shadow Hunter**

***Book 1 of Rosie O'Grady's Paranormal Bar and Grill***

*By BR Kingsolver*
*https://brkingsolver.com/*

*Cover art by Lou Harper*
*https://coveraffairs.com/*

*Copyright 2019*

***Get updates on new book releases, promotions, contests and giveaways! Sign up for my newsletter.***

# CONTENTS

*Here, Kitty Kitty*

*Bellator*

# PROLOGUE

I was almost fourteen and had just started my menses when my parents sold me to the Illuminati.

My parents didn't look at it that way, of course. What they saw was an adolescent girl bursting with power she couldn't control and they couldn't understand. The Masters promised they would train me, educate me, and raise me up through their hierarchy. Someday, they said, I might even reach the Council. Wealthy, revered, powerful.

As for me, I was buffeted by magic and emotions and feelings that I didn't understand. Alternately exultant and terrified, I had no idea from one moment to the next whether I might be wracked with pain as I tried to contain more magic than I could hold, or suddenly find myself able to walk through walls and stop time, or lie helpless and weak in the aftermath of a magic attack that wracked my body and mind.

And so, for the next five years, I studied and trained —twenty hours a day—until my Masters judged me fit and safe to turn loose in the world. I trained in weapons, martial arts and magical arts, and built my body and stamina with athletic training. I also studied the theory of magic, history, art, philosophy, political science, and practical chemistry and physics. As a woman, I also studied the arts of flirting and seduction, for the Illuminati believed that all weapons should be mastered.

I joined the Hunters' Guild, the organization within the Illuminati that protected us and fought against the evil in the world.

For that is what the Illuminati stood for. The shining Light that stood against encroaching Darkness. We held back the demons and Dark sorcerers. We hunted down the rogue vampires and werewolves and other creatures of the Dark. We sought out the sorcerers in their shadow worlds and purged them from our reality. We protected humankind from the nightmares that without us would crush all that was goodness and Light from the world.

Master Robyn and Mistress Chantelle honed me into a weapon that even the Illuminati had never seen before. They called me Scorpion because of my fast reflexes and deadly strikes. In the dance of death, I tested at the top of all my talents—first among all the Hunters who had ever come before me. And on my nineteenth birthday, they gave me my first assignment.

Two weeks later, five evil men who controlled immense power within the United States government were dead. The catastrophe they steered toward was averted. Humanity survived, never knowing how much of their freedom and happiness was due to the Illuminati watching over them.

I continued to train and hone my skills. I gained in power. The Guild sent me on missions alone that would normally be assigned to teams of five or more. I triumphed over the oldest and most powerful vampire in Austria, destroying his nest and scattering his children who survived. I fought a snow dragon to a standstill and sent it back to its cold northern lair to lick its wounds for another Age. I hunted down sorcerers and evil acolytes of the Dark forces and dispatched them.

---

Master Benedict, The Illuminator and head of the Council, called me to his office. I had been his apprentice since graduating from my training, and it was he who had raised my awareness and skill with my magic to new heights. He had also seen to my advanced training in the carnal arts, teaching me techniques that could be used for bewitchment, infiltration, and assassination beyond anything I could have imagined. I had no idea why such an exalted leader would reach out to a young, untried woman such as myself, but every day I counted myself fortunate.

"I have a special assignment for you," Master Benedict said. "A man named William Strickland, an industrialist and a sorcerer deeply immersed in the Dark Arts, has created a powerful weapon. The only purpose for this weapon is to strike against us, for only we stand against him and his goal of world domination."

My Master provided me with the information I would need to find Strickland and presented me with a plan for gaining access to him.

"Be extremely careful," he said. "Strickland is powerful and canny. This dance will end with one of your deaths, and you must ensure that death is his. Once you have accomplished that, you must take possession of the weapon he has created and bring it back to me."

He took a drink from the jeweled cup on his desk and seemed to study me over its rim. "Strickland also has a daughter who is just coming into her power. Bring her to me, also, if you can. But if you can't, then you must kill her. He has already begun to train her in his Dark craft, and we cannot afford to let her grow to adulthood under any tutelage other than our own."

Strickland's financial empire had its headquarters in New York City, his chemical plants operated in Pennsylvania, and the man lived with his daughter in a mansion outside of Washington. I tracked him down and stalked him for weeks, learning his patterns, watching his movements, and searching for weaknesses.

His wife was dead, and other than servants, only his daughter and her nanny lived with him. Outside of his business, his only social contacts seemed to be a private gentlemen's club, which I quickly discovered was a cabal of like-minded mages. But Strickland was the leader, the strongest sorcerer of them all.

I first attacked that cabal, eliminating them one by one. My sword took the head of one, and poison in a favorite drink silenced another. A third had a weakness for young women, and in bed one night, I stopped his heart. The last two were riding together the night their car suffered an unfortunate accident.

By the time Strickland turned on the light in his study one night and found me waiting for him, he was alone and isolated.

"Who the devil are you?" he asked, throwing a spell at me that my ward easily deflected.

"Your time is done," I said. "The Illuminati have decreed an end to your Dark plans."

He blinked at me, then threw back his head and laughed. "*My* Dark plans? Oh, that is rich. The foremost arcane organization plotting world domination is going to stop *me*?" He sneered at me. "You Hunters have assassinated thousands of legitimate world leaders in government, the churches, and industry. You target any mage or witch working with the Light. The Illuminati have amassed incredible wealth that serves no purpose but to increase the power of its leaders."

Without warning, he hurled a bolt of energy at me. My ward absorbed it but was weakened. I leaped over the desk and swung my spelled sword. My adversary was much older than I was, and slower. He partially blocked the blow, but my backswing disemboweled him. He grimaced and clutched at his abdomen.

"The weapon," I said. "You built a weapon to attack us. Tell me where it is, and I will spare your daughter."

His eyes grew round, and he staggered back against the wall. "Leave her alone," he said between clinched teeth.

"The weapon."

He gave me a pained smile and shook his head. "Only the Illuminati would consider it a weapon." He motioned with his chin toward a ball of crystal the size of my fist sitting on a small pillow on a shelf. "It shows truth. Look through it when a man speaks, and it shows his lies. Look at a spell or a book or a work of art to see how true it is. Watch an Illuminati ritual and see the blood and the Darkness hidden beneath the surface. Yes, take that to your masters, and they will destroy it. But in the process, it will destroy them."

Strickland laughed then and slid down the wall to sit on the floor. I walked over to the shelf and picked up the crystal, then turned back toward him. When I held the ball up in front of me and looked through it at him, I saw that he was dying. I also saw that he was a wizard of the Light, and felt, though I couldn't tell how, that everything he had told me was truth. Shaken, I tucked the ball in my pocket and turned to leave.

As I walked down the hallway, a young girl stepped out in front of me. Her long red hair looked as though it was blowing in a breeze, but I felt no wind. Her green eyes seemed to blaze.

"Are you the Scorpion?" she challenged me.

"Yes."

She bit her lip, and when she spoke again, her voice trembled. "Have you already killed him? He said you would come, and you would kill him."

"He may yet still live," I said, "but he is dying."

"And you have the crystal?"

"Yes."

"Then you need this as well," she said, holding out a book. Old and leather-bound, at least three or four inches thick, it must have been heavy from the way she struggled to hold it.

"What is it?"

"A book," she said, with a brave grin. "You do know how to read, don't you?"

I closed the distance between us. She faced me bravely, her eyes darting only once to my blade dripping her father's life blood. I took the book in my other hand and discovered it was even heavier than it looked. I glanced down at it and almost dropped it.

The book was black leather trimmed in gold. The

title, in the secret language of the Illuminati, said, "The History of the Illuminati."

"Read it," she said. "He said—my father said—that you must read it." She gave me a grin that was so malevolent I took a step back. "They will kill you when you take it to them, whether you read it or not. I hope you're stupid enough to believe their lies."

She whirled and walked through the wall. I leaped after her, but the wall was solid, and I could find no hidden latch or door, and following blindly would be folly.

---

Completely unsettled, I took the book and the crystal to my hotel. I opened the book to find it was written by hand in the language of the Illuminati. The first entry was dated in 1308 AD. It told of the formation of a secret Order, attracting many mages in various countries. They used the Order to connect and communicate with each other, to share knowledge and to provide strength for mutual protection.

Above all, the Order was formed to protect its members against the Church and European royalty. Phillip the Fair of France had recently destroyed the Knights Templar, arresting its members and seizing its treasure. In particular, the Order's members were concerned about the Inquisition, which had executed many witches and mages.

Turning to the back of the book, to the last entry, I recognized the familiar neat handwriting of Master Benedict, the Illuminator. The date was three years before I acquired the book. Satisfied as to its authenticity, I sat back and began to read it from the beginning. Within the first twenty-five pages, a sense of dread began to form in my mind.

By the time I finished the book, including the few notations about me, my training, and Benedict's plans for me, I had raged many times. In the end, I felt numb and empty. Not only had I been duped, I was complicit. Rather than being a force for the Light, I had advanced the reach of the Dark.

The City of the Illuminati sat on top of a small mountain in a forest in the northern part of the United States. Only one road led to it, and no one except those deeply immersed in the lore of the Illuminati knew it was there.

A month after I killed William Strickland, I walked into Master Benedict's office and placed the small crystal ball on his desk.

"This is the weapon Strickland created," I said. "It sees through mendacity, and only truth can be seen if you look through it. The ultimate lie detector spell. If I look through it at a person who is not healthy, it shows his disease. It discloses the lies of politicians, clergy, and used-car salesmen. If I use it to read a book, it tells me what is fact and what is fiction. A very, very dangerous weapon."

Without another word, I turned and walked out of his office. I continued out of the palace at the center of the City, through the streets, and out the gate in the outer wall. All I took with me was a small backpack with water, some food, some money, and a large black-and-gold book. My weapons I left at the gate, for I had no desire to continue the life I had led. The path of the Illuminati was mine no longer.

I walked for an hour, and then the earthquake started. I turned and looked back at the shining City of the Illuminati on the top of the mountain behind me. The light fluctuated and the City shook. A haze passed over the sun, turning it red. The rumbling grew in volume until it sounded like a freight train only a few feet away.

I stood, stunned, staring at the City, unable to move.

The City exploding caught me off guard, and a minute later the shock wave knocked me off my feet. The City was on fire. It burned for hours, well into the night, but never spread past the outer wall. The City sat at the junction of two major ley lines, and those rivers of magic fueled the flames. I watched it, my emotions a confused jumble.

Many of the people who died that night had been kind to me. Yes, they had lied to me and manipulated me, but I couldn't help but feel that some of them had loved me in their own way. I grieved for the thousands of souls consumed in those flames. Everyone I knew was dead. But I also grieved for my own soul, shattered beyond any hope of redemption, or at least that's how I felt at the time.

In the morning, there was no trace of the City. I climbed back up the mountain and found nothing to indicate it had ever existed. Not a brick, not even a speck of ash. The only home I could remember, the place where I grew up, was gone. The mountain looked as though it had never been touched. The road I had traveled the day before was also gone. A game trail going in the same direction as the road was the only break in the virgin forest. I realized I was alone in the world, and a wave of emptiness and regret washed through me.

I knew my blackened soul should have perished with all the others, but I was too much of a coward. I wanted to live, but I didn't know why, or what I would do. I didn't know where to go, but only that I had to get far away from that place. There were still Illuminati loose in the world. If they ever found me, ever found out what I had done, they would hunt me down and slaughter me. And if anyone ever suspected I had the book, nowhere would be safe for me.

For the book contained the secrets of the Illuminati —all of them. Their rituals, their spells, the locations of their treasure. Someone could reconstitute their evil using that book. I had tried to burn it, and it wouldn't burn. I could bury it, but if anyone found it and could read it, then the Illuminati might rise again. I couldn't let that happen.

I turned down the game trail and followed it for three days until I came to a little-used road. I followed that road for another three days before I came to a small town.

A bus came through that evening, and I took it going west.

## CHAPTER 1

The bus dropped me off a little before midnight, and the station was almost deserted. A single ticket window had a light, but no one was behind the counter. Two or three people slept in chairs. It was impossible to tell whether they were waiting for a bus or were homeless and wanting a little warmth. I pulled a city map from a stand and turned toward the exit.

There wasn't a person in sight on the street. Yellow streetlights reflected off the wet pavement, but no lights showed in the windows of the surrounding buildings.

I studied the map. The two most notable features were the ocean on the west and the river bisecting the city into northern and southern portions, with a dozen bridges spanning the divide. To the north, the city was bounded by foothills that I knew turned into tall, white-topped mountains, but I couldn't see that in the dark. The bus station was in the southwestern part of the city, in a warehouse district.

According to the map, a two-block walk should take

me to a main street running from east to west, and I hoped there would be some cheap hotels somewhere around there. It was probably too much to wish for, but I thought it also would be nice if the area had an all-night diner. It had been a long time since breakfast.

I had traveled over three thousand miles in less than two weeks, ending up two thousand miles from where I started. When I left the City of the Illuminati, I was dressed in Hunter's garb—skintight, all-black ballistic cloth. The first city I arrived in, I bought a suitcase and some other clothing at a thrift shop before taking another bus out of town.

I had done my best to obscure my trail, going west to Kansas City, then south to Dallas, then northwest to Westport. No one knew where I was, and no one had any reason to connect me to that part of the country, let alone to Westport. I knew no one there, and I had never been there before.

During my trip across the country, I had constantly looked over my shoulder, afraid that someone would recognize me. My guilt weighed heavily, not only for my treachery against the Illuminati but also for all the murders I had committed. Before I read the book, those had never bothered me, but now faces haunted my sleep.

Normally, I paid attention to my surroundings, but bone-tired and relieved to finally reach my destination, I didn't realize I had company before he grabbed me. With one hand over my mouth and his other arm around my chest, he dragged me backward into an alley. His face loomed over me, his fangs barely visible in the gloom as he lowered his face toward mine.

His expression changed to one of shock as he flew

across the alley and slammed against a wall. The bricks cracked, as did his bones, and his body slumped in a heap in the filthy muck on the pavement.

I was acutely aware that he could identify me if he ever saw me again. That thought sent a wave of panic through me. If even a rumor of my magical skill reached the Illuminati, it might trigger their curiosity. I pointed at the vampire's head and said a Word. His skull soundlessly exploded.

Clutching my handbag, I picked up the small suitcase I dropped when he grabbed me and hurried away. I cast a protective shield around myself, then ventured out of the alley, hoping that no one had seen me kill the vampire. I hurried away, my stomach turning flip-flops from the adrenaline roaring through my system. Even though I was the only person on the street, it felt as though a thousand eyes were watching me.

The map turned out to be accurate, and the street I sought was far more alive than I had hoped—a couple of motels, a movie theater, a sex shop, half a dozen bars, and lots of bright lights. A couple of the bars were obviously strip joints, but even those looked fairly clean and not too sleazy. There were people out on the street, and not all of them appeared to be hookers or their customers. For a red-light district, it was one of the nicest and most respectable I thought I'd ever seen. I still wasn't inclined to try the nearest motel that advertised rooms by the hour.

The sex shop, strip bars and hookers were all to my right. To my left, the bars looked more like regular establishments with a mixed-gender clientele. I could see skyscrapers in the distance, maybe a couple of miles away, and I knew from my map that beyond downtown was the harbor. I took a deep breath and walked left.

The bars definitely started looking more respectable the farther I walked, including a couple of nightclubs with valet parking. After a while, the sign for another hotel appeared. I didn't see any restaurants still open, but as I crossed the street to the hotel, I saw a sign on a place a few buildings down a side alley. Rosie O'Grady's Bar and Grill. Hoping their kitchen was still open, I walked on past the Huntsman Hotel and pushed on the door. As I did so, I saw a small hand-lettered sign that read, "Bartender wanted. Inquire within."

A tingle passed through me as I stepped over the threshold, but before I could react, I was inside. I found myself in a typical Irish pub with subdued lighting, dark wood, exposed beams, a long bar backed by an impressive array of bottles, and a limited set of taps. The place was larger than it looked on the outside, with at least fifty tables in the main room. About half of the tables were occupied, and off in one corner, several people were throwing darts. Near the dart players, a couple of guys were shooting pool on one of the two tables. Past the pool tables, a smaller room had a flat-screen TV hanging on the wall. The smell of food made my mouth water.

The bartender waved at me. "Seat yourself," he said. He was a large man, bald on top, with mutton-chop sideburns, wearing a white shirt and an unbuttoned dark vest showing a prodigious stomach. He looked like he had stepped out of Central Casting.

Making my way to a table by the wall, I sat down and a waitress appeared. She was in her late forties, medium height, and a bit overweight, with dark blonde hair falling out of a bun.

"What will ye have?" she asked in an Irish accent, slapping a menu down in front of me.

I glanced at the menu and saw the beer list in one corner. Less than a dozen choices, and all of them Irish.

"A Smithwick's, please."

"I think we still have some of the salmon that's on special," she said, and turned away to head for the bar.

I looked around. It was after midnight, and several people were eating. The food looked good. When she came back with my beer and a glass of water, I asked, "Are you still serving the full menu?"

"Aye. We don't close the kitchen."

"What's closing time here?"

"The law says two o'clock for places that sell liquor. We don't pay any attention to that since our clientele doesn't pay any attention to normal hours."

I remembered the tingle I felt when I walked through the door. "The Guinness stew, please," I said.

She shook her head. "Ye really don't want it. He'd be scraping the bottom of the pot this time of night, and the fresh batch isn't ready yet. Do ye like salmon? I'll give it to ye for the price of the stew."

She really wanted me to order the salmon. "Yes, please. Thank you." I would have eaten the scrapings, or the menu, if that was all they had.

She grabbed the menu before I could try it, though, and took off in the direction of the kitchen. I gratefully sipped my beer, leaned back in my chair, and felt some of the tension drain out of my shoulders and back.

The special turned out to be a poached salmon filet with tarragon sauce, accompanied by fingerling potatoes, stewed apples, and asparagus. It smelled wonderful, and I couldn't remember when I'd last had such a meal.

The waitress sat it on the table, and asked, "Can I get ye anything else right now? Another beer?"

"No, I'm fine. I saw a posting for a bartender when I came in."

She glanced down at my suitcase.

"New in town?"

"Straight off the bus. Would you recommend that hotel on the corner?"

"I wouldn't recommend it, but I wouldn't warn ye against it. This time of night, it's probably better than searching for something else. I'll send Sam over when ye finish eating."

I took my time, savoring every bite. What kind of hole-in-the-wall pub served a gourmet meal in the middle of the night? I also studied my fellow customers. They were an eclectic lot, and some were dressed rather eccentrically. Capes and cloaks were long out of style, but some people always affected out-of-date fashions. The crowd in Rosie O'Grady's seemed to be trying to revive them.

A couple of the women knocking down a pitcher of dark beer looked like hippie earth mamas, while the women at the table next to them would have been at home in an Edwardian drama. Across the room sat two couples who were obviously stuck in the punk seventies. A man wearing an expensive business suit sat with a short, pink-haired woman in a low-cut blouse and a miniskirt who was reading his cards. A guy who looked like a biker appeared to be having an earnest conversation with a clean-cut man wearing black plastic-rimmed glasses and a tweed jacket with elbow patches.

That tingle when I entered the pub made me wonder what kind of place I had wandered into.

I pushed the empty plate away from me and took a pull on my beer. No sooner did I set the glass on the table than the bartender dropped into the seat opposite me. He was even larger close up. With him seated across from me, I had to look up to see his face.

"Jenny said you enquired about the job," he said. "Do you have any experience?"

"Yes, but I'm afraid I can't supply you with any references."

He nodded, looking at my suitcase and appraising my clothing. "I don't ask many questions," he said. "I don't need to know why you're here, but I do need to know one thing. Is the law looking for you?"

"No."

"Understand something. If you work for me and I ever find out you've lied to me, I'll kill you."

Well, that was blunt enough. I believed him. "Then I might have to leave some questions unanswered," I replied, "assuming those questions are ever asked. I won't steal from you, and I won't lie about anything to do with my job."

"If you can't answer a question, we'll figure out where to go from there. Don't ever lie to me. And anything that happens in this establishment stays here. You don't discuss my business or my customers outside."

"Understood."

"Come mix some drinks for me," he said and stood up.

I followed him behind the bar, hung my coat on a

hook he indicated, and rolled up my sleeves. He handed me an apron and I put it on. I was a little above average height for a woman, but I barely came up to Sam's chest.

"Look around, see how things are laid out," he said.

I did. Garnishes, syrups, bitters, liqueurs, glasses. Something about the arrangement of the bottles in the well bothered me, and without thinking, I straightened them out, then realized what I had done.

I shot the bartender a look, but he only nodded and said, "Make me an old fashioned."

Half a dozen drinks later, he said, "I've seen enough. You can handle the basics without thinking, and that's all I'm looking for." He motioned to a battered recipe book in a corner by a cooler. "If it gets more exotic than that, the customer better know how it's made. I'm Sam O'Grady, and I own the place. I need someone to work Thursday through Sunday evenings, five until two, plus I may call you in occasionally. Fifteen bucks an hour, no time and a half. All tips go into a pot to split with the entire crew at shift's end. When can you start?"

"Is this a pretty standard crowd?" I asked.

"For this time on a weekday? Yes. Dinnertime is busier. Dawn until eight o'clock is busy. Lunch is busy. Weekends are busier."

"Do you have bouncers?" I asked. Sam was large enough to toss a drunk elephant out on its ear, but if I had a problem, I wanted some help.

His brow furrowed as he looked down at me. "You need a bouncer?" Reaching under the counter, he pulled out a sawed-off baseball bat. "Someone needs bouncing, bounce them with this."

He shoved it in my hand, and I almost dropped it

when I felt the surge of magic from it. I realized he was watching me closely, and I was sure my expression gave me away.

"Like I said, I don't ask too many questions. But you found the door and managed to walk through it, so I don't think I have to explain what this is," he said, taking the bat from me. "You have a beef with a customer, everyone who works here will back you up, and probably most of the regulars. Where are you staying tonight?"

"I planned on going to the hotel next door."

Sam nodded and handed me a business card. "Tomorrow, go see this lady and tell her you're my new bartender. Come in at four to take care of the paperwork."

I didn't recognize the address, of course, but it read, "Springfield Apartments, Eleanor Radzinski, Leasing Manager."

"What's your name?"

I thought furiously, then decided to use a name I hadn't used in a very long time, one that, to my knowledge, no one was looking for. I even had legitimate ID for it buried somewhere in my purse. "Erin McLane. I didn't say I'd take the job."

He simply stared at me with a raised eyebrow.

I gave him a half-smile. "I'll take the job. Thank you."

For the first time, he smiled. "Welcome aboard, Ms. McLane."

CHAPTER 2

The hotel wasn't bad—fairly clean and affordable. It also had hot water that didn't run out, and I stood under the shower for half an hour before going to bed. I took another shower when I woke up in the morning.

Sam mentioned the bar being busy between dawn and eight, so I figured it served breakfast. I felt somewhat reluctant to go back there, however, so I had breakfast at a diner down the street. While I ate, I went through the help-wanted section of the local newspaper. That was somewhat depressing and made me glad I found a job so quickly. It also made me wonder how and why I found a job so quickly.

It wasn't that there weren't any jobs, but there were few jobs I could reasonably apply for. A couple of bartender and waitress jobs, but most businesses were hiring professional positions that required degrees and references. Then there were jobs for delivery drivers, construction workers, and dock workers. I didn't know what it took to be a dock worker, but doubted I had the requisite physique.

My training as an assassin involved intensive attention to various insertion strategies. I knew how to dress for and interact with the so-called cream of society at the fanciest country clubs and charity functions, but I also learned to tend bar and wait tables. No one paid attention to the caterer's hired help, and what better way to get inside a billionaire's security? But none of that came with a certificate of completion, and my formal schooling in the conventional sense had ended when I was fourteen.

I found the Springfield Apartments on my map, and the waitress directed me to a bus stop. Standing out on the street, I read the rest of the paper while I waited. I didn't see any stories about vampires assaulting women in dark alleys. Maybe the guy who attacked me was new in town, too.

The bus took me directly to my destination without a transfer. It was only about half a mile, so I could walk to work without a problem. The apartment complex had four buildings, each with twelve apartments, four on each of the three floors. Eleanor Radzinski was a neat, petite blonde in her fifties, casually dressed in khakis and a white long-sleeved blouse. She was also a witch. I could feel her magic.

"Sam at Rosie O'Grady's recommended you," I said. "I'm new in town, and he hired me to tend bar."

Radzinski nodded, taking in my clothes and my lone bag. "The apartments have a full kitchen, two bedrooms and one bath. All of them are the same. No furnishings. Five hundred a month plus a hundred for utilities," she said. "Two hundred damage deposit. There's a laundry room in the basement of each building. Parking is free, but you've only got one extra space for guests."

I filled out the paperwork and bit my lip as I dug out my money. I hoped I made decent tips, or it was going to be a hungry month.

"Ms. McLane."

I looked up from counting the money.

"It's a week into the month, so four hundred fifty total, and I'll accept Sam's judgement on your character in lieu of the damage deposit."

I kind of stared dumbly at her for a minute, trying to process what she said and the kindly expression on her face. My eyes got a little blurry, and I glanced down quickly. Kindness wasn't something I expected. "Thank you."

"I have a couple of vacancies," she said. "Do you want a ground-floor apartment or third floor? There aren't any elevators."

That would make it difficult hauling furniture up to the third floor, but I didn't have any furniture, or money for furniture, so it really didn't matter that much. I looked out the window. The apartments on the second and third floors had small balconies.

"Third floor, please." The first floor struck me as far less secure than those on the upper floors.

She took my money and gave me four keys. "Two for the outside doors and two to your apartment," she said, and led me to the building next door to the office. One of my keys opened the outside door, then she led me down a long hall to another door at the far end.

"Your key works on this door, too," she said. "You can use either the front stairs or these back here."

We climbed to the third floor where I used another

key to open the door from the hallway. I was surprised at how spacious the place was. Kitchen, small dining nook, living room with sliding-glass doors leading to the balcony. The bedrooms weren't large, but they weren't cramped, either, and the bathroom was nice, with both a bathtub and a shower.

"If you decide you want a roommate," Radzinski said, "you'll have to pay another two hundred deposit, and if you get a pet, that will be a two hundred deposit. Familiars count as pets." Obviously, I wasn't the only one able to detect magic.

She handed me a piece of paper with an address on it. "Goodwill. You can probably find what you need to furnish it there. A bed, at least, and what you need in the kitchen."

"Thank you," I said, thinking that I might also be able to find some clothes that fit. I only had one set of clothes I could wear for work, and that would be noticeable pretty quickly. Working in restaurants wasn't the cleanest work in the world.

After she left, I opened the door to the balcony and stood against the railing looking around. A tree-lined stream ran behind the apartments, and sort of a park about fifty yards wide, with walking or jogging paths on both sides. It would be quiet, and I was glad she had put me in the back, away from the street and the parking lot.

A trip to Goodwill took a chunk of my remaining cash—the amount the damage deposit would have cost me—but it bought a bed, a set of sheets, a blanket, and a pillow. The sales lady helped me pick out things she said I would need, and I ended up with four matching plates, four mismatched mugs, four glasses, four bowls, a six-person set of flatware, a cast-iron skillet, a saucepan, a spatula, and a large wooden spoon. Two pairs of black slacks and four simple blouses completed my purchases.

I had never lived on my own. My apartment in the Illuminati's palace was more like a fancy hotel room with servants who cleaned and served my meals. On missions, I stayed in hotels.

As I left Goodwill, the lady said, "We don't carry cleaning supplies, but there's a hardware store up the road."

I hadn't even thought of that. She gave me the address, but I didn't have enough money left to spend on luxuries. I figured I could probably last the week with the soap and shampoo I'd taken from hotels on my journey, and use my tip money later to get whatever cleaning supplies I needed.

Goodwill promised to deliver the bed the following day, and I hauled the rest of my loot back to the apartment. I put the clothes in a washer in the basement, took a shower, then went back and put my laundry in the drier. When it finally dried, I had barely enough time to dress and catch the bus to work. And considering the storm that had blown in, I was happy to have the bus.

Something Sam said the previous night seemed strange—"...you found the door, and managed to walk through it..." I kind of thought I understood the second part. That tingle I felt when I passed over the threshold.

I stood at the corner by the hotel and looked down the alley. In daylight, I couldn't see the bar's sign. Walking down the alley and standing directly in front of the door, I could easily read the sign over it, bold white letters against the brick background.

There weren't any lights. The night before, the sign

had been lit up and stood out from the wall. But as I looked at it, that was impossible. The words were painted on the bricks, and there weren't any lights. At all. Of any kind.

The tingle was still there when I pushed through the door. I had encountered warded veils intended to keep some people or creatures out, while allowing others in, and they felt like that.

A tall, very thin man stood behind the bar. His black, messy hair made his pale complexion stand out even more. Simply based on coloration, he could have been my brother. He watched me walk up to the bar without any change in expression.

"Is Sam here?" I asked.

"Yes."

He didn't say anything else, change his expression, or give me any other indication he was alive and cognizant.

"I'm Erin, the new bartender."

Still nothing. Eerie.

"Would you please tell Sam that Erin is here?"

He turned and walked to a door down by the end of the bar and knocked. The door opened and Sam came out.

"Thank you, Liam," he said, smiling at the statue standing in front of him. Then he looked my direction. "Hi, Erin. Come on back."

I glanced over my shoulder as I followed Sam through the door and saw Liam still standing there, staring out at the room.

Past the door, Sam pointed to a stairwell on our right going down. "That's the storeroom, and the tap lines run down there to the kegs, so you don't have to haul them up. There's an old-fashioned lift in the alley, a big dumb waiter, actually, that lowers the deliveries down there."

His office was larger than I expected, and neater than I expected. He sat behind the desk, and I took a chair in front of it. The standard new-hire paperwork sat there waiting for my signature.

"Did you find a place to stay?" he asked.

"Yes, thank you. Ms. Radzinski is very nice."

He nodded. "You'll see her in here. She mostly comes in on your shift."

When I dug out my identification the night before, I discovered the driver's license was expired, and not in my real name. But I had procured a passport in my real name when I was nineteen, and that was valid. Had it only been nine years since my old life ended? A lifetime ago. Then, three weeks before, I had walked—run— away from the new life I had so arrogantly embraced and ended up in Sam's bar.

Sam raised an eyebrow when he looked at my passport, and I guessed it had to do with my age, or maybe the four-year-old picture. People always told me I looked older than I was. He didn't say anything, though.

I finished signing everything, and Sam made copies of my passport and social security card. He handed them back to me and pointed to a sign on the wall.

"That's posted at both ends of the bar, but you probably didn't notice it."

### Rosie's Rules
*Cash only—no cards, no checks, no promises*
*No display of weapons*

*No loud arguments*
*No fighting*
*No release of bodily fluids*
*No conjuring*
*No bewitching without the subject's permission*
*No shifting*
*All artifacts must remain secured*
*NO POISONS, POTIONS, INHALANTS or EXTRACTS not*
*sold by the bartender*
*Killing a paying customer will result in a lifetime ban*

"I am dead serious about these," he said, "and I expect you to enforce them, using the minimal amount of force necessary."

I stared at him with my mouth open for a moment, then said, "The door."

He nodded. "That door is almost invisible after dark. In fact, the whole alley is dark unless you have a magical ability. And the ward on the door prevents most people from coming in at all.

"The tingle," I said.

He was quiet, then his eyes widened, and he leaned forward. "The tingle?"

"Yeah, I feel a slight tingle—I don't know, a slight buzz maybe—when I cross the threshold."

"That's all you feel?" His voice grew louder.

I suddenly felt self-conscious. "Yes. Is there supposed to be something else?" I shrugged. "Maybe the spell is getting old and needs to be renewed."

"My bloody-red ass it does! That warding spell—" he sputtered, then said, "the only person who feels a slight tingle is me, and I cast the damned spell."

I tried to shrink down in my chair. "I'm sorry," I said

27

in a barely audible voice. "I'm probably just describing it poorly. How do other people describe it?"

Sam was clearly upset, and I didn't completely understand why.

"People without talent get a feeling of dread, which confuses them, so they can't remember why they're here, or why they want to come in. If they try, it causes dizziness and nausea. For people with talent, most describe it as having to push through resistance. Jenny says it's like walking through a wall made of honey."

"Oh."

He studied me for a while, then said, "There's a cop, a sensitive without a shred of talent, who comes in here. I guess it feels different to different people. Well, Liam said he would stick around an extra hour in case you have any questions, and I'll be here another couple of hours. Jenny's working tonight, and Dworkin is in the kitchen, so you should be all right. Welcome aboard."

"Uh, Liam."

"Yes?"

"What's wrong with him?"

"Oh, yes, I guess I should explain about Liam. He's a great bartender and knows about every drink anyone ever invented. He's autistic, and he's not very social. He doesn't ask questions, and he doesn't deal with change very well. Don't ever yell at him, and if you get frustrated, take a moment and think about what *you* need to do to fix the situation. He answers questions, but you have to make sure what you've said is a question and he knows it's aimed at him. If you ask him if he knows how to make a Singapore Sling, he'll say, "Yes." But if you want him to make one, you have to tell him to make it. If you want him to tell you how to make one, you have to say, "Liam, please tell me how to make a Singapore Sling. And for God's sake, don't tell him to do anything *to* anyone. If you want someone bigger than you thrown out, ask anyone but Liam. I can't afford the repairs."

Sam stood and started around the desk. "Liam doesn't work alone. Either I'm here, or he works with another bartender. He'll be your second on our busiest nights, and you'll be glad to have him. Come on, and I'll introduce you to the staff who are here."

Steve Dworkin, six feet and slender, with sandy hair and beard, was the cook. He smiled and welcomed me, then turned back to the grill to turn a steak.

Donny, last name not spoken, was the dishwasher and kitchen help. "If someone orders food from the bar," Sam said, "Donny will bring it out for you."

Jenny Rafferty and Emily Watson were the waitresses on duty that night. With the bar open twenty-four hours, seven days a week, I was told the total staff numbered almost thirty, some part time.

When I expressed my surprise at never closing, Jenny said, "If we were closed, where would our customers go? Where would ye have gone? This is more than a business, it's a safe place."

## CHAPTER 3

L iam was easier to work with than I feared he would be. If I did exactly what Sam had told me, being careful about how I phrased things, Liam answered every question I asked. By the time he abruptly informed me that his hour was up, took off his apron, fished his share of tips out of the jar, and walked out without saying a word of goodbye, I had a pretty good handle on where things were and how the place worked.

The one unusual thing was the small refrigerator under the bar with small bottles of neatly labeled potions, inhalants, and extracts. They all seemed to have a beneficial purpose, though I could see that a few had a recreational purpose as well. Thankfully, there weren't any poisons.

Five customers sat at the bar, four of them either eating dinner or munching on an appetizer, and two-thirds of the tables were occupied. Jenny and Emily—a pretty strawberry blonde about thirty years old—were handling the dinner rush without even seeming to hurry. I had seen Emily carry two enormous trays of food out of the kitchen, leave one of them floating in the air while she served a table from the other tray, then recover the floating tray to serve a different table. Obviously, Sam knew his clientele. No one batted an eye at Emily's trick.

Sam came out of his office around seven o'clock.

"Go take your break and get something to eat before I leave," he said. "Just tell Dworkin what you want. You can sit at the end of the bar."

I ordered the Guinness stew I missed out on the night before and looked over the specials sheet while I ate. Jenny came over and leaned against the bar, surveying the room.

"Things going okay?" she asked.

"Yes," I said. "You folks have made it rather easy. Is Steve married?"

Jenny erupted with laughter. "Ah, wouldn't it be nice to have someone at home who cooks like that? As a matter of fact, he is in a triad with a woman and another man, but ye never know, they might be open to new blood."

I felt my face warm, and Jenny laughed harder.

"Dworkin is probably the best," Jenny said, "but all of the cooks here are better than average. Ye'll never get a bad meal at Rosie's."

It got busier as the night wore on. Fewer people ordering food and more ordering drinks. I kept busy, but never felt overwhelmed.

At a little after ten, the pink-haired emo lady I had seen reading tarot cards the night before came up to the bar and stuck out her hand.

"I'm Lizzy," she said. "Some people call me Dizzy Lizzy cuz I'm kinda ditzy sometimes."

I smiled and shook her hand. "I'm Erin."

"You're new in town?"

"Yes. Brand new."

She nodded. "I thought so. I was born here, and I never saw you before. If there's anything you want to know, just ask. You know, about the city," she turned and cast a glance around the bar, "or the people, or if you want a reading."

"Thanks. I will."

She seemed to study me, but about the time I started to grow uncomfortable, she said, "Sloe gin fizz, please."

I mixed her drink and collected her money, then watched her wander off toward a table where a man wearing a long black cape and a top hat was sitting alone. She sat down with him and pulled out her cards. He reached into his hat and also pulled out a pack of cards. They both began laying cards on the table, seemingly ignoring each other.

Before I could try to figure out what they were doing, the outside door opened, and two young men and a woman walked in. The storm obviously hadn't abated because they wore rain ponchos dripping water. They took them off and hung them on pegs by the door, then one of the guys and the woman walked toward the bar. The second guy made a motion with his hand, spoke a couple of words, and the water they had dripped on the floor disappeared. He looked up and saw me behind the bar, smiled, and followed his friends.

"What will you have?" I asked. All three looked to be in their middle to late twenties.

The first guy stared at my chest and licked his lips.

He was tall, over six feet, with red hair cropped short, hazel eyes, and a muscular physique. In all, rather pleasant to look at. When he didn't answer, I turned to the woman.

"Can I get you a drink?"

"Guinness and a shot," the woman said. She was shorter than me and almost skinny, with long, full red hair, a narrow face, and a million freckles.

"A shot of what?"

She looked a little surprised. "Jameson's, of course."

I gave a sigh. Sam's lineup of Irish whiskeys was impressive, and only one person all night had ordered anything other than the cheapest.

"I'll have a rusty nail," the first guy said.

"I'll have a black and tan," the second guy ordered. He winked at me. Shorter than his friend, with medium-length brown hair, he was good-looking enough to model.

I moved down the bar and began pouring his drink.

"Nice ass," I heard the redheaded guy say. I knew he said it loud enough for me to hear on purpose. A part of me wanted to take him by the throat, and another part of me cringed at my reaction. I wasn't a Hunter anymore, and I needed to learn other ways of dealing with people. I was sure that Rosie's Rule about not killing paying customers applied to the bartender as well as the customers.

I slid the shot and mixed drink across the bar while I waited for the Guinness to settle, then finished the beers.

"Five, ten, and five," I told them, facing each in turn.

As they shelled out their money, the first guy said, "You're new."

"Yup. Born last night." I looked at the five he handed me, then looked up at his face. He smirked. I smirked back. If the guy wanted to be an asshole, that was his right, but I didn't have to serve him with a smile. I put their money in the register and the tips from the other two in the jar, then walked away to where another customer stood waiting.

A few minutes later, I looked up and saw just the shorter guy standing there. The redheads had found a table across the room. I walked back over to see if he needed anything.

"I'm Trevor," he said, pushing a dollar bill across the bar. "Josh can be kind of an ass sometimes."

"Erin. And the rest of the time he's the sweet, generous guy I met tonight?" I didn't take the dollar. Trevor glanced down at it, then back up at me. I shook my head. "A word of advice. Guys like that never have your back when the rubber hits the road. All they think about is themselves."

"You're kind of young to be that cynical. Josh really is a good guy."

"You're kind of old to be that naïve," I said, and walked away.

Around midnight, I felt a strange wash of magic from the front door. A man in a long raincoat came in, shook himself, and hung the coat on a peg where it dripped water onto the floor. He walked over to the bar, his shoes squishing. He wore a dark business suit, a white shirt, and a tie. His skin was a Mediterranean olive shade, and his dark hair was very short on the sides, with sort of a flattop. If Sam was the innkeeper from Central Casting, I decided this guy must be the cop that Sam had mentioned.

"Good evening," he said.

"Good evening. What can I do for you?"

"Hot coffee."

I went and poured a cup. The pot was about five hours old, as I was the only one drinking it, but I didn't see any need to make a cop feel any more welcome than I had to.

"You're new," he said when I pushed the cup across the bar. I took the two dollars and rang it up, then gave him fifty cents in change.

"I get that a lot," I said. "There are some very observant people who come in here." I had heard that about fifty times that night, and it was starting to get on my nerves.

Out of the corner of my eye, I saw that Jenny was leaning against the far end of the bar watching us.

"I was wondering, you didn't happen to come into town last night, did you?"

I was trained too well to react, but inside, I readied myself for action. Someone would have found the vampire and probably reported him to the police.

"I don't remember," I said. "It's such a welcoming place that I feel like I've been here all my life."

His face tightened.

"It was just a question," he said.

"And I don't answer personal questions from people I don't know, especially from policemen who don't identify themselves."

He straightened, reaching inside his jacket and pulling out his ID. "Detective Lieutenant Jordan Blair. And you are?"

"Erin."

He waited, but when I didn't volunteer my last

name, he finally gave up. "Did you come into town last night, Erin?"

"Yes, I did." I almost chuckled, realizing that Liam had the perfect tactic for dealing with cops and lawyers."

"The reason I'm asking is a man's body was found a few blocks from here this morning. Between here and the bus station. You didn't happen to see anything unusual last night, did you?"

I shook my head. I wasn't sure what was usual. I had been in cities where vampires munching on the locals was quite common. "Is it unsafe to walk around here at night? I have to take the bus home after my shift."

"It might be best to have an escort wait with you at the bus stop," he said.

I caught myself biting my lower lip and stopped it. "Thank you. I'll try and take that advice. No one told me this is a dangerous neighborhood."

"Well, I wouldn't go that far. It's normally pretty safe." He looked around the room. "There are some interesting characters who hang out around here, though."

"Really? Such as?" I leaned forward over the bar and craned my neck, looking back and forth over the crowd of wildly eccentric people I had been serving all evening. One guy near the dart boards was juggling three glasses full of beer. The remarkable thing was that he wasn't using his hands, the glasses just floated around in a circle without spilling.

He turned slowly and kind of blinked at me. I tried to give him the most wide-eyed and innocent expression I could manage.

Blair stuck around for a few more minutes drinking

his coffee, then put on his raincoat and ventured back out into the storm.

"What did he want?"

I jumped at Jenny's voice right next to my shoulder.

"Dear gods. Make more noise when you sneak up on me," I said.

She chuckled.

"Asked if I saw anything unusual last night. He said they found a body between here and the bus station this morning."

Jenny nodded. "I heard. A vampire. I guess he ran into a meal that bit back."

"Do you get a lot of that around here?"

"Not just around here. For the past year, it seems a lot of vamps, wolves, Fae, and other types of rogues have decided to make this city their home. Used to be they stayed pretty low key, but the past few months it seems to be getting out of hand." She sort of pointed across the room. "The biker with the red bandanna around his head? He's a werewolf. Works as an accountant downtown. Been coming in here for years without causing any trouble, but he told Sam there's some new kids in town who are troublemakers. Best to be aware of your surroundings when you get off at night."

As it turned out, I didn't have to ride the bus. Steve Dworkin drove right by my apartment complex and dropped me off on his way home.

CHAPTER 4

Lieutenant Blair came in earlier the following evening. His tie was loosened, and he sat on one of the barstools instead of leaning against the bar as he had the previous night. He surprised me by ordering a beer.

"Off duty, Lieutenant?" I asked as I put it in front of him. "Would you like to see a menu? Special tonight is smoked-haddock pie with potatoes and Gubbeen cheese." I had tried it for my own dinner and fallen even more in love with Dworkin. I found myself thinking that I shouldn't dismiss that group marriage thing so quickly.

Blair blinked at me. "Is that an Irish dish?"

"Rosie's is an Irish bar," I said. "Next best thing to being there."

"Sure, I'll try it."

I put in his order and gave him a place setting. As I started to walk away, he said, "There was another murder last night."

"Oh? I caught a ride home with the cook."

"Guy was beheaded," Blair said.

"Is that how the other guy died?"

He shook his head. "We think he was shot. Striking similarity between them, though. They both had very strange teeth. Almost like fangs."

I laughed. "Maybe you've got vampires."

Blair didn't laugh. "What would you know about vampires?"

"About what I know about werewolves, garden gnomes, and leprechauns. Shall I ask around and see if I can find any vampire experts for you to talk to?"

Emily signaled for my attention, and I went off to fill her drink orders. I didn't care for the way Blair continued to watch me, though.

"Is he always like this?" I asked Emily. "Just come in and watch people?"

"He's not watching people," she said. "He's watching you. I think he likes you."

I gave her a fake shudder. "Just what I need, a cop who's fifteen years older than I am. Why can't I attract what I really want—a millionaire in his nineties?"

She laughed and took the drinks to her customers.

Steve came to me around midnight and said he needed to leave early. I told him that I'd catch a bus, but Blair's warnings echoed in the back of my head.

When Jill, my replacement, came on at two o'clock, I gathered my jacket and set off for the bus stop. The rain had slacked off to a light drizzle. I stayed alert, paying special attention to the alleys and side streets.

I only had to wait for about five minutes once I reached the bus stop. When I got off at my apartment, even the drizzle had stopped. I started off across the compound for my building when I heard the scuff of a shoe behind me. Picking up my pace, I rounded the end of a shoulder-high hedge and almost ran into someone.

The man in front of me reached out, and the footsteps behind me picked up speed. I felt a hand on my wrist, but I pulled away before he could grab me. Dropping into a crouch, I pulled energy from the nearest ley line, then leaped straight up, my balled fists shooting out and catching my attacker under the chin. As he fell away from me, I smelled the alcohol on his breath. Not a vampire, just a common drunken mugger.

I dropped back into a crouch and spun around with one leg extended, catching the other guy at the knees and sweeping him off his feet. A couple of kicks to the heads of both muggers, and it was over. I surveyed the unconscious men on the ground, conflicted over whether I should call anyone.

"I'll call the police," Eleanor said, her voice from the darkness causing me to jump.

"Will I have to talk to them?" I asked, thinking about Lieutenant Blair.

"No, I'll just tell them I have a couple of homeless guys trespassing and want them gone. My tenants need to feel safe."

"Thanks."

Standing in the shower a few minutes later, I wondered how much Eleanor had seen and whether she would mention the incident to Sam. I was quite aware that most young women couldn't have subdued two large men so easily. When I walked away from my previous life, I thought I had walked away from violence. Yet, I found myself repeatedly having to defend myself.

Did everyone live that way? Was the world really that violent?

---

The following day, when I got to work, Jenny and Sam were standing at the end of the bar talking. They looked up when I came through the door and continued to watch me as I hung up my coat and put on an apron.

"What's up?" I asked.

"Another beheading," Jenny said. "A vampire was found this morning near your apartment complex."

"Oh. I had a run-in with a couple of muggers last night, but neither of them was a vampire. Eleanor said she was going to call the police, but I didn't talk to her this morning."

"Jenny told me that Blair has been around," Sam said. "We thought you should be forewarned if he came in again."

I nodded. "Thanks. He acts like I'm somehow connected to these vamps, but Jenny said the problem started a long time ago."

"That's true," Sam said, "but the bloodsuckers getting killed is new. The beheadings are definitely new. Makes me wonder if there's a Hunter in town."

Jenny shrugged. "Tales me gran used to tell. Leprechauns and banshees and Hunters. Not that I'm skeptical about things I ain't never seen, but I'm believing more in some kind of gang war between different vampire gangs."

I couldn't stop thinking about Sam's comments as I went about my work. Beheading a creature wasn't easy, and who carried a sword capable of beheading a human or vampire? No one carried a sword around in public. Except a Hunter, with a spelled blade no one could see.

And if there was a Hunter in the city, would it be one who knew me? As the Illuminator's Hunter, I never worked with other Hunters, and except for those who trained me, no one knew me well. And while there were Illuminati strongholds scattered around the globe, I had never visited any of them.

Almost everyone in the Order I had ever met was based in the City of the Illuminati, and everyone in the City was dead—almost five thousand people incinerated when the Illuminator destroyed Strickland's truth crystal. The entire Council, all the Masters, and the Commanders of the Hunters' Guild. The heads of the regional headquarters in Germany, England, Russia, and Ecuador weren't Masters, and never would be. All of the Masters had risen through the Hunters' Guild, and only Masters were elevated to the Council.

My first impulse was to pack up and run, but there was a problem with that. All the money I had was a couple of nights' tips, and I was eating all my meals at work. I didn't know how far a bus would take me on the money I had, but it would be a hungry trip.

Even if I did run, the chances of me running into a Hunter at my next stop were still greater than zero. I couldn't run forever, unless I wanted to run forever. But would I survive an encounter with a Hunter? I had thrown all my weapons away. Sure, I had my magic, but all Hunters were mages. Had I run all that way to Westport only to find myself cornered and out of options? I felt really young, all of a sudden. Young, and clueless, and wishing someone older and wiser could tell me what I should do.

"Are you all right?" Sam's voice startled me out of my reverie.

"Sure. I'm fine."

He seemed to be studying me, and I felt my face grow a little warm.

"You don't know anything about these vamps, do you?"

His voice rang in my head, *Never lie to me.*

"The beheadings?" I asked.

Sam nodded.

"No." I took a deep breath. "I've heard of Hunters, and that would certainly fit. I mean, who carries a big-ass sword around beheading people? But I always considered meeting a Hunter to be as likely as meeting an Elf."

Sam chuckled and I relaxed a little. "Seen some strange things in my life." He gestured to the painting of Rosie that hung on the wall. "She claimed to be part Elf, which I guess would mean I've got Elf blood. But I've never met one."

I blinked at him, then turned to give the painting a closer inspection than I had before. Sam looked nothing like the woman in the painting, although Jenny had told me that Rosie was Sam's mother.

"How do you know the muggers you met last night weren't vampires?" Sam asked.

I turned back to him. "Alcohol on their breath. One of them anyway. They were slow, too."

"Yeah, we don't do much business with vamps. They don't drink booze, and we don't serve blood. One will come in with a girl once in a while so she can get something to eat. I don't encourage it."

43

Blair showed up after midnight looking tired.

"Coffee or a beer, Lieutenant?" I asked.

"Beer and a shot," he replied.

After a few days, I had figured out what people expected for that order. I poured his drinks and set them in front of him.

"Something to eat? Or are you drinking on an empty stomach?"

He gave me a hard look, but it softened when I didn't flinch. "I should probably eat something."

"Stew," I said, and walked away to put in the order.

He called after me, "Suppose I don't like stew?"

I gave him a wink. "Momma knows best. Shut up and eat what you're served."

"You're too young to be a mother."

"You're too tired to argue with me."

He chuckled. "You got me there."

Donny brought the stew from the kitchen almost immediately. I took it and set it down in front of Blair just as the door opened and the group I'd labeled the three mouseketeers came in—Josh, Jolene, and Trevor.

"Hey, pretty lady," Josh almost shouted. "What's shakin tonight?"

Even with the bar between us, I could smell his breath. "Got a special on coffee," I said.

"Coffee? Hell, I don't want no coffee. Gimme a rusty nail."

I looked over at Jolene and Trevor. Jolene swayed a little, but Trevor looked like he still had some of his faculties.

"Why don't you guys get a table and I'll bring your

order out to you?" I suggested, looking at Trevor directly, then shifting my eyes toward Blair.

"Just tryin to get rid of me?" Josh asked.

"Providing extra-special service," I said.

"Come on," Trevor said, grabbing both of his buddies by the arms and dragging them away.

Blair looked up from his dinner and watched them go, then looked at me.

I took a deep breath and turned into the kitchen.

"Steve, I've got a couple of drunks out here that I don't want to serve," I said.

"Regulars?" he asked, flipping a burger, then looking at me.

"Josh, Jolene, and Trevor. Trevor looks okay, but the other two are wasted, and Josh's getting belligerent."

Dworkin sighed. "Let me show you a trick." He took me back out behind the bar and opened the small refrigerator. Picking up a potion bottle, he said, "Put half of this in Josh's drink. He'll be asleep in five minutes, and then we can call a taxi for him."

I looked at the label. VHH. "Won't hurt him?" I asked.

"Nope, but don't let the cop see you do it."

I also cut the rusty nail half-and-half with cola, figuring Josh was so out of it that he wouldn't notice. I poured the other half of the potion in Jolene's beer. Trevor had taken my advice and ordered coffee.

Emily came up to the bar and said, "Are those special for our problem children?"

"Yeah. I told them I'd bring their drinks out to them."

She nodded. I picked up the tray, and as I crossed the room, I noticed that she paralleled me, stopping out of Josh's line of sight and about five feet behind him.

"Last call," I said as I set their drinks on the table. "I think you guys have had enough fun for the night."

"Nope," Josh said. "Not as much fun as I could have with you."

As I put Trevor's coffee on the table, Josh reached around, grabbed my ass, and squeezed. I straightened and looked down at his drunken smile. I smiled back and reached for his wrist.

"I'm not going to break it," I said, holding his wrist in my hand. "But the next time I will. Do you understand me?"

The tables around us grew quiet, but Josh didn't notice.

"Fine piece of ass." He squeezed harder—hard enough to hurt. "When do you get off? I wanna get off, too."

I popped him on the head with the tray I was holding in my other hand. It sounded a little like a cheap gong. His eyes crossed, he let go of my butt and swayed in his chair. I bent over until my face and his were only inches apart.

"Next time, I break your wrist," I said, and hit him with the tray again. He slid out of his chair under the table. I looked up and said, "Emily, can you please call Josh a taxi? I don't think he should be driving. Jolene? You going to split the cab with him?"

"Uh, yeah. Yes ma'am."

I looked at Trevor, who gave me a bit of a smile as he took a sip of his coffee and shook his head. "I'll take the bus."

I put Jolene's and Josh's drinks back on the tray and

took them back to the bar. A lot of the other customers were clapping and cheering, and my face felt like it was about to combust.

"I don't think you'll get much crap from now on," Steve said as he ducked into the kitchen.

"From anyone," Blair said, holding up his shot in salute and then downing it.

## CHAPTER 5

Before he left, Blair dropped the fact that another vampire had lost his head, and two werewolves were found in the same condition. He didn't use the terms vampire and werewolf, of course, but I figured it out from his description of the victims.

"It seems all the murders are being committed between closing time and dawn," Blair said.

I gave him a long skeptical look, then said, "I guess that narrows it down to a bartender, a waitress, or a taxi driver. Just look for someone carrying a guillotine around."

He gave me a sour expression in return.

"Seriously," I said. "Have you ever tried to cut the head off anything? A chicken, a rabbit? It isn't easy. Do all the dead people know each other? Are they part of the same criminal gang or something?"

"You ask questions like a cop."

I laughed. "I just watch too much TV." Which was a lie. I didn't own a TV or a computer. Just nine years of Hunter training with the Masters giving me random pieces of information and telling me to put the picture together. And why in the hell was he coming around talking to me about murdered vampires?

"Lieutenant Blair, why are you coming around talking to me about this shit? Do you think I get off work and go hunting for people with fangs?" I shook my head. "I'm truly baffled. Do I look like the kind of person who enjoys beheading people?" I threw up my hands and said, "Hell, do I look like the kind of girl who gets off on talking about that kind of gruesome shit? I need to work on my image."

He had the good grace to look embarrassed. He put his head down, looking at his lap, but he didn't answer me. What Emily said earlier popped into my brain.

I leaned across the bar. "If you want to ask me out, making me feel like a suspect is the wrong way to go about it. I'm really a normal girl. Talk to me about flowers and bunnies and sunsets."

I was about as far from normal as a girl could be, but an article I read in a magazine at the bus station in Dallas said I should have goals. And living a normal life sounded like a great goal to me.

Blair's head popped up, and he gave me a deer-in-the-headlights look. I turned and walked away, back into the kitchen where I didn't have to deal with him.

"What's up?" Steve Dworkin asked.

"Getting away from the cop," I answered. "I don't know what his problem is."

Dworkin snorted, and Donny made a rude gesture with his pelvis.

"Thanks, guys," I said. "That's just what I need after dealing with Josh tonight."

They both blushed and I lost it.

"How the hell would you like it if a bunch of drunk, horny fools came back here and started fondling you? Well?" It only took three steps for me to push Donny against the wall, my hand on his crotch. "You like it? You like having someone force themselves on you? Feels good to get groped, doesn't it?" His expression told me all I needed to know.

Whirling about, I was on Steve in an instant, bending him back against the grill, my hand squeezing his crotch hard and my mouth against his. "Feels great, huh? Like a dream come true. Gee, ain't it great to have a woman jumping your bones?"

I stepped back. They stood frozen, their expressions shocked.

"Think about it," I said. "I put up with that shit every night, and everyone thinks it's funny. Jenny and Emily put up with it. It isn't funny. Fuck you. Fuck men. Fuck the world. You're lucky I don't start killing people tonight, because I'm tempted."

I spun around and went back to my station behind the bar. Blair was still there, his money sitting on the check. I picked it up and rang up the transaction, then gave him his change with the receipt.

"I apologize," Blair said. "I didn't mean to make you feel like I suspected you of anything."

I was still pissed off. "Suspected? Like suspected that I might say yes if you asked me out? Or suspected I might be a serial killer?"

He stared at me for a moment, then said, "If I suspected you would say yes, then I would ask you to dinner on your next night off. But so far, you haven't given me any clue that you might be interested."

"And so far, neither have you."

We stood there staring at each other, and I gradually realized that we were being stupid.

"Dinner at Delmonico's? Tuesday night?" he asked.

I realized that my mouth was hanging open. I shut it.

"No," I said. I took a couple of deep breaths, backing away from him. "Lieutenant Blair, I normally don't date customers, and I don't even know you." Hell, I had never dated anyone unless I intended to kill them. I stared at him and couldn't figure out what to say. Did I want to make things so final? "But that doesn't mean that I'll never say yes."

A slight smile softened his face. "Fair enough. Good evening," he said with a bow.

I watched him collect his coat and walk out into the night. He had left his change on the counter, which was a lot more than a normal tip.

What in the hell was I doing, I wondered? I had never had a real date in my life. I knew how to seduce men, but I didn't know the first thing about relationships —at least about the emotional part. I understood all the mechanical parts. How to dress, what to say, when to make my moves to advance whatever agenda I was pursuing.

Was I supposed to be in love to go on a date? Did it automatically mean sex? What did you do in the morning when the man was still alive? You'd probably have to talk to him. What would you talk about?

I went home that night a complete mess, my mind as confused as I could ever remember. Freedom to be yourself and do whatever you wanted was a very chaotic way to live. No wonder the world was so screwed up. Who was I, and what in the hell did I want to do? So far,

I had simply run away from my past, but what was I going to do with my future? I was used to a lot more structure. Day-to-day decisions weren't something I had been trained to deal with.

And on the other hand, I was scared something fierce of anyone telling me what to do. Nine years of being a 'good girl' and following orders proved that my sense of who to trust couldn't be trusted. Was I simply gullible? Naïve? Or maybe just dumb? I wanted to trust Sam, and I wanted to trust Blair, but how was I to know if that was the right thing to do? Every way I turned seemed to present some kind of danger. Sometimes I just wanted to give up, but I didn't know how to do that, either.

When I arrived at work the following evening, I went into the kitchen. Steve and Donny gave me guarded looks.

"Hey," I said. "I want to apologize for last night. I was way out of line."

I saw them relax, then Donny said, "No, you weren't. I was. I'm kinda clueless sometimes. Sorry."

Steve chuckled. "Hell, you were gentle with us. When I went home and told my old lady, she reamed me out good. She's still pissy about it this morning. Naw, we were the ones out of line. I know how hard it is dealing with drunk assholes, and it's worse as a woman. I guess we just needed a little reminder."

Trevor came in alone around six. He sat at the bar, ordered a beer, and asked for a menu.

"I apologize about last night," he said when I sat his beer down.

"Oh. Was that you grabbing my ass? I thought it was Josh."

"Well, yeah, but—"

I leaned over the bar. "Why do you constantly feel the need to apologize for him? I mean, if you're worried that people will lump you together, you're right. Apologizing for him won't help that, Trevor. You hang around with a jerk, people are going to assume you're a jerk, too."

His face turned bright red. "You don't understand."

"No, I don't. Why don't you explain it to me? Use small words. I'm only a girl."

I thought his face couldn't get any redder, but it did. "I've known Josh since grade school. When kids used to pick on me, he defended me. And now we're in business together."

"Trevor, you don't owe him. I know you think you do, but you don't. And if you think your business is going to do well, I hope you're the one dealing with customers."

He handed me a card. *Lost and Found.*

"That's the name of your business?"

Trevor nodded. "We find things."

"Tell Josh to find a clue," I said. "What do you want to eat?"

The rest of the evening went fairly smoothly. Trevor sat at the bar and we chatted for more than two hours. He told me some funny stories about things *Lost and Found* had been employed to find, and I enjoyed it. I found myself wishing that he'd come around without

53

Josh more often. I was sort of dreading having to face Blair again, but he didn't come in on my shift.

As I was packing up to go out to the bus stop, Lizzy came over. "Hey," she said. "I have a group of friends who get together for brunch every Sunday. A lot of them are people I've known since high school. Would you like to come? Give you a chance to meet some people."

I was sort of stunned. Making friends was as foreign a concept to me as dating. I had sort of a friend for a couple of years when I first went to live with the Illuminati, but she died in a training accident. Or so I was told. "Uh, sure. I guess. Where is it?"

Lizzy gave me the address. "We meet up around eleven," she said. "I'll give you my phone in case you have trouble finding the place."

She stood there with her phone in her hand looking expectant. I wasn't sure what to do, so I grabbed a pencil.

"Okay."

"It would be easier to just tell me your number. I'll call you, and then we'll have each other's numbers."

"I don't have a phone."

Her expression didn't change at first, then she blinked, then said, "Oh, did you lose it? Wow, that's a bummer." She gave me her number, and I wrote it down. "Let me know when you get your new phone," she said and smiled. "See you in the morning."

As I watched her walk away, I realized how lonely I was. Lizzy reaching out to me, Eleanor's and Sam's and Jenny's kindness were foreign. They knew nothing about me, about what a horrible person I was. I wondered how they would react if they did.

I walked out of the bar at two-thirty in the morning and found Jolene leaning against the wall across the alley. Without a word, she fell into step beside me.

"Hi," I said.

"We need to talk."

"Okay."

We walked around the corner and down the street a ways before she spoke again.

"I don't want to see Josh hurt."

"Oh? Well, the easiest way to prevent that is for him to keep his hands to himself."

Jolene shook her head. "That's not what I mean. He's falling for you and I don't think—"

I stopped. I realized I was staring at her with my mouth open, so I shut it. I couldn't think of anything to say. She was several steps down the street before she discovered I was no longer with her. She turned back to look at me.

"What is he, twelve years old?" I asked. "I like her, so I call her names and hit her? Dear gods. Between you and Trevor, he doesn't have to take any responsibility at all, does he? Can he even wipe his own nose?"

She started to open her mouth, but I closed the distance between us. "Don't worry about your little boy's feelings. If the son of a bitch touches me again, I'm going to put him in a hospital. As for any kind of romantic attachment, I'd rather date a cockroach. I'll sleep with a vampire before I sleep with him."

Furious, I stalked away from her. Worried about poor little Josh's feelings? She would be better served worrying about his breathing, and whether he would continue to do so.

Josh reminded me so much of a boy, young man, I

55

knew when I was sixteen. Roger was a Hunter trainee a couple of years older than I was, and he took an interest in me. He was cocky and a bit of a bully. He made my life miserable, grabbing my ass or my breasts, trying to get me alone and force me to kiss him. I complained to my Masters about him, but they just told me he had a crush on me and 'boys will be boys.'

On his first mission, Roger went to Mexico with three older Hunters to take down a rogue werewolf pack. The others returned, but Roger had disobeyed orders, gotten separated from his brethren, and the shifters killed him. I had always thought that if the Masters had slapped him down and held him accountable when he was younger, he might have learned enough discipline to save his life.

I arrived at the bus stop to discover the street light that hung over it was out. Not only that, but I saw the taillights of the bus fading into the distance. I was late, and it would be half an hour until the next bus. Then I heard a noise from the bushes ten feet away. I cautiously moved closer and saw a woman's foot sticking out from the foliage, twitching and sort of kicking.

Rushing forward, I met my second vampire. He had a girl pinned on the ground with his hand over her mouth and his head lowered to her neck. Her eyes were round with fear, and when I came into her field of vision, she began struggling harder.

I kicked him in the side, and he turned his head toward me. I kicked him in the face and cast a spell that pinned him to the ground. Grabbing the girl by the arm, I pulled her away from him. There was a little blood on her neck, but I couldn't tell how much he had drained her.

He probably hadn't done much yet, because she was plenty animated and actively using her limbs to get away from him. The lassitude normally associated with the vampire's saliva entering her bloodstream hadn't kicked in yet.

"Scream," I told her as she staggered away. "Call the cops." Then I turned back to the vamp. I wasn't sure what to do with him. Killing him with a witness present wasn't a good idea. Actually, considering Detective Blair, killing him wasn't a good idea at all.

The girl definitely wasn't hurt too badly because her scream about deafened me.

I took the vampire by the ankles and dragged him close to a nearby tree. Taking a good grip on his ankles, I swung him around in a circle, lifting him off the ground, then stepped toward the tree. The jolt of his head against the trunk jarred him loose from my grip, and he fell to the ground. As far as I could tell, he was unconscious, so I dissolved the holding spell.

Turning around to head back to the bus stop and check on the girl, I saw her leaning against a man who had his arms around her. And then I saw his face. Blair stared at me with a shocked expression.

"Hi, Lieutenant," I said. "Can I borrow your guillotine? I seem to have forgotten mine."

He seemed to choke, then took a deep breath. "Ms. McLane. Do you think you can take this young lady to my car while I handcuff the man you just brained?"

"Sure." I walked up, put my arm around her shoulders, and guided her toward the bus stop where a tan sedan sat with its lights on and its engine running. I opened the back door and guided her into the seat, then glanced back at Blair and the vamp. It looked as though Blair handcuffed him and left him on the ground.

"Where are you coming from?" I asked the girl.

She named one of the strip bars and said she worked there. Blair reached the car at the same time as a regular cop car pulled up. He spent a couple of minutes talking to the cops, who then dragged the vamp to their car and put him in the back seat.

"I need to take a statement from you," Blair told me after he finished with the uniformed policemen.

"Yeah. I heard noise in the bushes when I came to the bus stop," I said. I pointed to the broken street light. "He had her pinned down and was biting her neck."

Blair nodded, making notes in a little book. "And what did you do?"

"I kicked him a couple of times, then dragged her away from him."

"And picked him up and bashed his head into a tree," Blair said.

"I didn't want him to attack me."

"Of course not. Do you mind telling me how you managed to pick up a two-hundred-pound man and swing him around like he weighed nothing?"

"I work out. He doesn't weigh nothing. He's actually pretty heavy."

He stared at me as though waiting for me to say something else. Finally, he said, "You work out."

"Yeah. I like to stay in shape."

## CHAPTER 6

Blair took the stripper to the emergency room on the south edge of downtown, then drove me home. I suppose I shouldn't have been surprised that he didn't ask me my address, but I was. Obviously, he was watching me. But it didn't explain why he drove right past my apartment while taking the stripper home, then back the way we'd come to take me home.

"I'll need you to come down to the station tomorrow and give a formal statement," he said when he pulled up in front of my apartment building.

"I gave you a statement."

"Yes, but I'll need one on the record. I may have more questions for you."

I glanced at him, trying to figure out whether he was just trying to get more time with me or what he really wanted.

"He bit her on the neck," I said, and watched for his reaction.

"I noticed that."

"I didn't see his mouth," I said. "Was this one of your guys with funny teeth?"

He gave me a long look, then said, "Do we have to play these games?"

"I don't know what you mean."

"You're what, five-seven, five-eight, and a hundred thirty-five, forty pounds? You kicked a two-hundred-pound man's ass. Picked him up like a child and slammed his head into a tree. That's not normal. Men with fangs biting women in the neck is not normal. Why don't you tell me what's going on?"

"I've been in this city less than a week, and you want *me* to tell *you* what's going on? If you're so smart, I think you can figure out what's normal and what's not. I'm tired, Lieutenant. Unless you have some basis for keeping me up all night, I'm going to take a shower and go to bed."

He didn't say anything.

"Good night, Lieutenant," I said, opening the door and getting out of the car.

Blair watched me unlock and go through the door of my building. I climbed the steps to the second floor and stopped to watch through the window on the landing as he drove away, then I continued up to my apartment.

As I crawled into bed, I wondered if every city on the continent had a rogue vampire problem, or if I simply got unlucky in my choice of a place to live.

It felt as though I had barely fallen asleep when the cheap alarm clock started ringing. At first, I couldn't figure out what the noise was. When you don't go to work until five o'clock in the evening, you usually don't have a problem getting up on time.

When I turned it off, the little Disney girl on the clock face reminded me of Lizzy and her brunch. Blair had dropped me off at five-thirty in the morning and I'd only had four hours of sleep. I considered rolling over and going back to sleep. But Lizzy had reached out twice, offering friendship. So, I dragged myself out of bed, took a shower, and put on my one dress.

I took a good look at myself in the mirror as I brushed out my hair and decided I should set aside a little money for some makeup—just for the eyes and some lip gloss.

When I walked into the restaurant, I spotted Lizzy immediately at a table with about a dozen young women. She saw me at the same time and waved, then jumped up and came to meet me.

"Most of these girls are norms," Lizzy said as she gave me a quick hug, "so be careful what you say."

She led me over to the table and pulled a chair in beside her while she introduced me. A waitress came and handed me a menu. I ordered coffee and orange juice.

I really didn't know what to expect, but the group was friendly, and other than a few questions that didn't get too personal, I was able to simply watch and listen. The conversations were mainly about their work, boyfriends, and things to do around town. Before I knew it, two hours had passed and some of the women started asking for their checks, paying, and heading out.

"So, what did you think?" Lizzy asked as we walked out to the parking lot.

"Seems like a fun crowd," I said.

"Yeah, they can be. I go out dancing with some of them occasionally, but we mostly see each other here on Sundays. With my classes and all, I don't have a lot of spare time."

"So, you're in school?" I asked.

"Yeah. I'm working on my doctorate in Astrophysics at the university."

I must not have kept a very good poker face because Lizzy laughed. "Yeah, Dizzy Lizzy can actually add two and two and integrate the sum into Einstein's theories," she said. "And I can cast a horoscope like nobody's business." Her expression grew somber. "One of the girls said there was a vampire attack near Rosie's last night."

"Yeah. He attacked a stripper at that bus stop a couple of blocks from Rosie's."

"Wow. Did she survive?"

I nodded. "The cops caught him. Do you know what they do with a supernatural?"

"They have a special jail," Lizzy said. "You know that detective who comes into the bar? The one who's got the hots for you? He's head of the Paranormal Crimes Unit."

I felt my face warm. "Blair?"

"Yes, that's the one."

"Sam said he didn't have any magic, but that he's sensitive to it."

Lizzy shrugged. "He doesn't seem to have any problem pushing through the veil. Maybe his magic is just dormant. Do you need a ride?"

She led me to a pink Mini-Cooper and unlocked the doors. "It matches my hair. Don't you think that's cool? Where to?"

I gave her my address, and she pulled out into traffic like a racecar driver pulling out of the pit.

"So, how did you know about the stripper?" Lizzy asked. "Did you see it?"

"I got to the bus late, or maybe it was early, and I heard something. When I checked it out, I found the guy biting her in the neck."

"Oh, wow." Lizzy shook her head. "You're brave. I would have picked up the phone." She glanced over at me. "Oh, yeah. No phone." Her eyes widened. "What did you do?"

With a shrug, I said, "Kicked him in the head."

We pulled up at a red light, and she turned to inspect me. "Yeah, I can see that. You don't have any soft magic, do you? It's all dominance."

She was right, I didn't have any soft edges. I was the girl the Illuminati sent out to pound their enemies into submission. I bit my lip, then said, "Not really. I don't have any talents, as people call them. I just tap a ley line and apply power to what I want to do. So, what are your talents?"

She chuckled. "I'm clairvoyant. A seer. But I see more than the future."

When my eyes met hers, I realized the depth that was in her, disguised by the pink hair, wild clothes, and colorful makeup.

"And that frightens people," I said.

She nodded.

"Truth is the most powerful weapon," I told her. Then I had a realization. "The cards. You really don't need them."

Lizzy blushed. "Well, they give me a medium to help express what I see. And it's less intimidating, I think."

"Don't look too hard at me," I said. "I'll just confuse you. Past, present, future—none of it is real. Even I don't know who I am."

"Yeah. I know."

———

Blair showed up shortly after I took over the bar that evening.

"You know, when I looked at that guy last night, half his head and his face was crushed," Blair said. "But this morning, all he has is a nasty bruise."

I nodded. "Vampires heal fast. You can find a lot of books about them at the library. Check the fiction section. Need a menu?"

He opened his mouth, and then closed it. I waited. Finally, I asked, "Coffee or a beer, Lieutenant? Menu?"

"You told me that you knew as much about vampires as you did about werewolves, garden gnomes, and leprechauns."

"Yes, I do. Tell me about the Paranormal Crimes Unit. What do you do? Investigate people for using a Ouija Board without a license?"

Blair didn't answer me, just stared with his mouth hanging open. I tossed a menu to him and went down to the other end of the bar to fill a drink order. I couldn't figure out what the guy wanted. He came around bugging me almost every night, asking weird questions, and evidently, following me around. I was tempted to assign Liam to wait on him when he came in but decided that Sam probably didn't want Blair interacting with Liam.

When I finished waiting on all my other customers

and filling the waitresses' drink orders, I came back to Blair. But just as I opened my mouth to ask him if he wanted to order something, I caught a glimpse of a couple in one of the back booths. They were young, and I'd noticed them when they came in. But what they were doing violated one of Sam's rules.

"Excuse me a minute," I said to Blair and rounded the bar. As I got closer to the young lovers, it became apparent that my suspicions were justified.

She lay back against the wall, a glassy look in her eyes. Blonde, but dressed as a goth. Her skirt was hiked up to her waist, but she wasn't protesting. He was the quintessential black-haired goth-dressed vampire, his hand was between her legs, and his fangs had already broken her skin.

"Hey! You can't do that in here," I said, loudly enough that he couldn't ignore me.

He turned his head, and his fangs dripped with her blood. "It's consensual."

"I don't care. House rules. Do it somewhere else."

"Fuck off." He turned back to his girlfriend, who was giving me a dirty look.

I grabbed him by the hair and dragged him out of the booth. He yelled, then started cursing me. He kept trying to grab onto something with his hands, or find purchase with his feet, but he couldn't get any leverage. I dragged him across the floor toward the doorway.

"Liam! Please open the door for me," I called.

He hurried around the bar and made it to the front door before I did. Out of the corner of my eye, I saw Blair standing at the bar watching me. When I reached the open door, I stopped.

"Liam, please throw this guy out in the street."

65

For the first time since I'd met him, I thought I saw a trace of a smile cross Liam's face. He reached down and grabbed the vamp by the neck and the butt of his pants, lifted him, and tossed him out like he weighed nothing. The vamp hit the street and skidded until he hit the wall of the hotel.

"Thank you, Liam. Please go back and watch the bar now."

He turned around and did as I told him. The vamp, on the other hand, sprang to his feet and acted like he planned to charge me.

"Don't even think about it," I told him, holding my hand out with my palm facing him. He took two steps and bounced off the shield I set in front of him. "Go away, or I'll call the cops."

"My girlfriend is still in there."

"And if she wants to go with you, she'll come out. But you are banned, buddy."

He snarled. I snarled back and closed the door. When I turned around, I ran into Blair, who was standing behind me.

"You'll call the cops?" he asked.

"Yeah. You should be good for something."

I looked over at the girlfriend and saw that Jenny was leaning over her. I approached them, and Jenny turned to me.

"She's at least two sheets to the wind," Jenny said. "I'm not sure she could rationally consent to her own name."

"I'll call a taxi if you can get her address," I said.

Jenny nodded.

After I called the taxi, I asked Blair, "Have you

decided if you're going to order something, or you're just going to warm the seat?"

"You seem to be able to handle vampires rather easily."

"Just a punk kid playing games and acting tough," I said.

I turned around and walked away, but halfway down the bar, I stopped and turned back. Blair irritated me, but he also scared me. I couldn't shake the feeling he was trying to pin the vampire killings on me. Why he thought I was at fault was a mystery.

"Lieutenant Blair, I don't know what your problem is, but me and my private life are none of your business, and I don't appreciate you badgering me or following me around. If you want to eat or drink something, then I will serve you. If you want to ask intrusive questions, I suggest you talk to the owner."

# CHAPTER 7

I came into work three nights later to find Sam behind the bar talking to Blair, who was sitting on a barstool. Both turned and watched me as I hung up my coat and tied on an apron. I wandered over and waited.

"That guy you threw out the other night was found dead last night," Blair said.

I looked up at Sam, waiting for him to say something.

"He was a vampire," Sam said. "They're already dead."

Blair shrugged. "We can't look at it that way. Vampires are a myth, like werewolves, garden gnomes, and leprechauns, so when we find a body, we treat it as a homicide. But someone thought he was a vampire. He had a wooden stake through his heart, and his head was cut off."

"Sounds classic," I said. "Have you rounded up everyone in the city named Van Helsing?"

Sam snorted.

"How many young women have you found with their throats torn out?" I asked. "Between that guy at the bus stop and the guy who came in here, you should be able to clear a few cases. Even vampires have fingerprints."

Blair looked unhappy and didn't answer me.

"I think it's a legitimate question, Lieutenant Blair," Sam said. "You've been in here after every vampire death, but my sources tell me that vampire attacks have escalated over the past three months. Who are you trying to protect?"

The cop turned and walked out. Sam and I looked at each other, and the expression I saw on his face mirrored my own feelings of puzzlement.

"How much does he really know?" I asked. "Lizzy told me he was with something called the Paranormal Crimes Unit."

A customer came to the bar and I pulled him a beer. Sam was still waiting for me when I finished.

"Blair doesn't report through the normal police chain of command," Sam said. "He reports to the District Attorney. I've heard of similar special units in other cities."

"So, how much does he know? You said he's a sensitive, but he doesn't have any magic?"

"I'm not sure exactly what he knows, or what he believes," Sam said. "I'm fairly certain that someone above him is a mage or some sort of paranormal. No one in the paranormal or supernatural communities wants the public to know we exist."

"And what is the difference between a paranormal and a supernatural?"

He gave me an odd look.

"Humor me. Couch, sofa, or divan. The words people use are confusing sometimes. I'm not from around here."

Sam chuckled. "Paranormals are humans with talents or magic—mages and witches. Supernaturals are non-human. Vampires, shifters, the Fae. Make sense?"

I nodded. "How many cops in his unit?"

"Maybe a dozen. Two witches, a couple of shifters, a clairvoyant, two or three mages. I'm not really sure about all of them, but some are normals. He also contracts with some freelancers. You've met Jolene, Josh, and Trevor. They do special jobs for him."

"And he's fixated on me because?"

"You don't seem afraid of vampires."

"So? Are you?"

He winked at me. "Not as long as I can see them coming. But I think Blair feels your magic. That you're strong enough to kill the bloodsuckers."

I threw up my hands in disgust. "Hell, half the people who come in here could kill a vamp. Some of them could poison a vampire with their blood alcohol levels." I held up the knife I used to cut up limes and other fruit. "Do you know how long it would take to decapitate someone with this? It takes five minutes to cut up a damned lime, and it's the only knife I have."

Sam shook his head. "Ask Dworkin to sharpen it. The other reason Blair's interested in you is that you showed up about the same time the beheadings started. One of the things he asked me is if I had ever heard of a being called a Hunter. Seems there have been a lot of vamps losing their heads in Dallas, Atlanta, and St. Louis as well."

"I tend to agree with Jenny," I said. "Hunters are

mythological, just like demons and angels. Humans haven't changed much over the millennia. We always invent fanciful stories for things we can't explain. And besides, Jenny told me the beheadings started before I came to town."

I was frustrated as hell. Westport had a vampire problem. I show up, and suddenly it was my problem. It wasn't fair.

Later that evening, Lizzy came in and made a beeline for the bar. Crawling up on one of the barstools, she leaned forward and said, "Erin, be careful."

"Oh? What's up?"

"I'm not sure, but something dangerous is going to happen."

"To me?"

She shook her head. "I don't know." Her face showed distress. "Either you'll be in some sort of danger, or something dangerous will happen around you."

I patted her hand. "Thank you for telling me. I promise, I'll be careful."

"You don't believe me." She scooted off the stool and started to turn away, but I held onto her hand.

"Lizzy, I take you seriously. I mean it. Thank you."

Her eyes got misty, and she blinked furiously, then said, "Okay. I just thought you should know."

"And I appreciate it." I fixed her a drink and refused her money. Whether she really Saw something or not, I wasn't in the mood to dismiss any warnings. Too much that I didn't understand was going on, and my own instincts were screaming warnings to be careful.

It also gave me sort of a warm feeling that someone cared enough about me to worry. My Masters warned me about all sorts of things, but they were more interested in losing an expensive asset than about whether I lived or died.

After the stripper attack, I was always very alert while walking to the bus stop, and with Lizzy's warning ringing in my head, I cast a personal shield when I left the bar. But that night the weather was nice and the walk and the wait for the bus were uneventful. The motion of the bus relaxed me, and I drowsed a little on the way home.

The bus always dropped me off half a block from the entrance to the apartment complex, but before I covered that short distance, three vampires stepped out of the shadows and stood in front of me. I could sense more of them behind me.

I had taken down one of the oldest and most powerful vampires in Europe, and I could feel the power of old vamps. The beings confronting me radiated none of that kind of power. They were young vampires, like the guy I threw out of the bar. Unfortunately, I had left my sword behind when I left the Illuminati. Decapitating a vampire with my fingernail would take even longer than doing it with the dull bar knife.

"Good evening, Hunter," one of the males said.

"I'm afraid you have me confused with someone else," I replied. "That's not my name."

"You're the bitch who threw Jimmy out of Rosie's," one of the females said. "Then you hunted him down and staked him."

"I threw a guy out of Rosie's, yes. But that's the last time I saw him."

"Someone is killing us," a male voice said from behind me.

"That might be because you're hunting and killing

innocents," I said. "Does your master know what you're doing? He can't be happy if you've drawn a Hunter to town."

The guy in front of me cursed. "We have no master. A Hunter killed him. The final death. And you're the number one suspect."

I wanted to roll my eyes. Did I have some kind of sign on my forehead that said 'vampire killer'?

"Just because I threw a vampire out of a bar?"

"Well, if you didn't kill him, at least we'll eliminate one vampire hater," the female said.

I fed power to my hands and feet as the vamps moved closer. Hands reached out for me, and someone behind me grabbed me by the shoulder. I punched the face of the guy directly in front of me, his face caved in, and he staggered backward. Dropping into a crouch, I wheeled around and extended my leg. The man behind me screamed and went down, his knee bent sideways.

One of the females grabbed my hair and pulled me off balance. My hand closed around her wrist and crushed it. She let go. I came up from my crouch and slammed my fist into her gut, feeling her ribs crack. She threw up blood and stumbled away.

A car engine sounded, and headlights shined in my eyes, outlining the vampires in front of me. The car rushed toward us, and the vamps turned to face it. A pink Mini-Cooper slid sideways, tires squealing, and hit two of the vamps, sending them flying.

"Get in!" Lizzy screamed.

I leaped toward the car, opening the door, but someone grabbed me from behind. I spun, elbowing him in the face, and lashed out with my foot, crushing his chest. As soon as he let go of me, I jumped in the car, and it accelerated away before I could even close the door.

We roared off down the street. Lizzy's eyes were wide, and I could smell her fear. The knuckles of her hands gripping the steering wheel were even whiter than her face. My own hands were shaking, so I didn't blame her.

"If you ever need a reference," I said, "I'll be glad to testify as to the accuracy of your predictions. I don't think they're following us, so you can probably slow down a bit."

A laugh exploded from her, and a few seconds later, she let off the accelerator.

"Damn! That was crazy!" She shot a glance at me, then looked back at the road. "Girl, you're hell on wheels when you get going!"

I had to laugh. "Liz, you're the one with the wheels. And thank you."

"So, what do we do now?" she asked.

I was buzzing with adrenaline, and her question caught me off guard. I wasn't sure what to do. "Well, it appears they know where I live, so that's out until dawn. Tell you what, let's go back to Rosie's and I'll buy you a drink."

---

We parked Lizzy's car, and I cast a ward around it. The car was much too noticeable, and I didn't want anyone trashing it, although I noticed a couple of dents in the side that hadn't been there the last time I saw it. I pointed them out to her.

"No biggie. I know a dwarf who runs a garage, and

he'll take the dings out in exchange for a reading," Lizzy said. "He's addicted to trying to win the lottery."

"Can't you tell him he's not going to win?" I asked.

She winked at me. "Oh, he wins a few bucks occasionally." She chuckled. "It all depends on what numbers he chooses, and how am I supposed to know that?"

When we walked into Rosie's, Jill, the overnight bartender, gave us a look.

"I thought you went home," she said.

"I thought so, too. Sloe gin fizz and a double of Redbreast," I said.

When Jill brought our drinks, I took a good swallow, then said, "I ran into a gang of vampires near my house, and Lizzy bailed me out. Figured it would be safer here until daylight."

Lizzy laughed. "As though you needed bailing out. Jill, she was *kicking ass*."

Trevor, Josh, and Jolene came over from where they were sitting. "Gang of vamps?" Trevor asked.

"Yeah. Six of them," Lizzy said.

"That's unusual," Jolene said. "They usually hunt alone."

I shrugged. "You know that guy I kicked out a few nights ago? Seems he got himself staked, and they decided I was the one who did it." I took another sip of my whiskey and shuddered at the burn as it went down.

"Were you?" Josh asked.

I gave him an are-you-really-that-stupid look. "Oh, yeah. When I get off work here, I'm always keyed up, so I go hunting vampires to burn off a little energy. And when I can't find any vampires, I wrestle with demons."

More people had come over and gathered around us.

"There is a rumor of a Hunter in town," Josh said.

Sliding off the barstool, I stepped before him, pulled my jacket open with my hands, and asked, "Do I really look like a Hunter? One of the baddest paranormals in anyone's mythology?"

Considering that the top of my head came to his chin and he outweighed me by at least sixty pounds, I knew I looked slight standing next to him.

Everyone laughed, and Josh looked sheepish.

"Well, Hunters are supposed to be strong mages."

"That's me! And since I don't have a big-ass sword, I just bite their heads off."

His face turned red at the laughter.

"To be honest," I said, "they fell prey to a pink Mini-Cooper. Left a couple of dents. If you don't believe me, go take a look at it. It's parked across the street."

That deflected everyone's attention to Lizzy, who told everyone how she had seen the vampires attack me and driven into them to rescue me. By the time she finished her story, someone had bought both of us another drink. A few people went outside and then came back, telling of the dents in Lizzy's car.

The conversation turned to the number of recent vampire attacks and theories about the vampire deaths. Some people agreed with Jenny that a vampire gang war was going on. Someone else said the vamps and the shifters were warring. And everyone had heard the rumor of a Hunter, but since no one had ever seen a Hunter, that theory gained little traction.

But I had to wonder. Someone with a very sharp or spelled sword was killing vampires. If it was a Hunter, then I was in danger as well. Not a very comforting thought. I downed the rest of my whiskey, and saw my hand was still shaking. Maybe the run-in with the vamps scared me more than I was willing to admit to myself. Or maybe it was the thought of a Hunter finding me.

## CHAPTER 8

At sunrise, Trevor drove me and Lizzy home in her car, with Josh and Jolene following us. I had lost track of how many drinks people bought me, and I certainly wasn't in any shape to drive, even if I had a license. Lizzy was close to being passed out.

I dragged myself out of bed around noon and went into work early so that I could talk to Sam. Of all the people I had met, he seemed to have the most common sense, and the most knowledge of the paranormal-supernatural scene in Westport. And in spite of myself, I liked him. I admitted that I might have some kind of weird daddy fetish, and was trying to substitute Sam for Master Benedict. But the fact was, I needed a sounding board. I had a lot of tactical experience, but my elders had always handled strategy, and I felt out of my depth. I hadn't mentioned my conversation with the vamps to anyone, but I wanted Sam's take on things.

He was behind the bar when I arrived, and I took a seat there.

"Heard you had some excitement last night," he said. "Hungry?"

"Yes to both," I answered.

He took my order for breakfast and sent it into the kitchen, then came back. I told him what had happened, including my short conversation with the vampires.

"They said that?" Sam asked. "They said their master was killed by a Hunter?"

"They think so. 'The final death' was the phrase he used."

"Damn." Sam leaned back against the back bar, one arm resting on his stomach and supporting his elbow, the other hand stroking his chin. After some time, he asked, "And he said they had no master?"

"That's what he said."

"Well, that's a shocker. The Master of the City, Lord Carleton, has been here since the late eighteen hundreds. He really was a lord, First Baron of Dorchester. Born in 1724. I don't know when he was turned, but supposedly it was during the Revolutionary War. He was in charge of all British armies in North America and was the Governor of Canada."

The kitchen boy came out with my breakfast, and Sam poured me a cup of coffee and a glass of orange juice.

"From what I know," Sam said, "a vampire that old could only be killed by a Hunter, a powerful mage, or another old vampire."

"And if another vampire did it, then he would inherit all the master's obligations and children," I said. "They would have a new master."

Sam nodded. "That's the way I understand it. Now, there are a few mages here with the power to contest him, but they never have. All the vampire attacks make sense now. The younger ones never have much control, and with no master, they're suddenly free to feed whenever and on whomever they want."

"Is this something Blair should know?" I asked.

He gave me a startled look. "I thought you didn't like him."

I shrugged. "I'd rather he leave me alone. But young vamps running around unsupervised in a city is like turning a bunch of children loose in a candy shop. Sooner or later, the newspapers and TV stations will get word of something going on and blow the roof off everything."

Sam sighed. "You're probably right. Hate to see Blair go up against a Hunter, though. He may irritate you, but better the devil I know than whoever would replace him."

---

Blair walked through the door at five-thirty, came directly to the bar, and sat down. Sam was still there, and I muttered, "I think an informer hangs out here."

"Why do you think that?" Sam asked, his face a perfect model of innocence.

"On duty, Lieutenant?" I asked. Blair nodded, and I poured him a cup of coffee and placed a menu in front of him.

"I heard you had some trouble last night," he said.

I turned to Sam and gave him a raised-eyebrow look, receiving a sour expression in return.

"Not at all," I said. "I finished my shift at two, then I

hung out until the sun came up, and there wasn't any trouble in here. Who did you hear it from?"

"There was an altercation involving a group of people in front of your apartment complex," Blair said.

"Really?"

Sam stepped forward. "Lieutenant Blair, are you aware that Lord Carleton is rumored to be dead?"

The shock in Blair's eyes told me he hadn't heard. He opened his mouth, then after nothing came out, he shut it. His eyes shifted back and forth between Sam and me. After a minute or so, he carefully asked, "When was this supposed to have happened?"

"Don't know," Sam said, "but I would guess it occurred around the time all the beheadings started. That would explain all the rogue attacks."

Blair shook his head.

"That would be before I got to town," I said, and stared at him, hoping to get a reaction.

"The vampires seem to think that the same person who killed their master is responsible for the deaths of their fellow bloodsuckers," Sam said.

Blair was silent for a bit, staring down at the menu. Then he tried to change the subject.

"I heard that a pink car ran into that group outside your apartment complex."

"I don't own a car," I said. Turning to Sam, I asked, "Do you know anyone with a pink car?"

Sam rubbed his chin. "My mum used to own a pink car. 1959 Cadillac. Sold it decades ago. God, was that thing a gas hog."

Blair gave up. "What's the special?"

"Baked chicken breast with either asparagus or snow peas," I answered.

He ordered it with the snow peas.

While Blair ate his dinner, Sam and I talked at the other end of the bar.

"One thing for sure," Sam said, "is you're not walking out of here alone anymore. If Dworkin can't give you a ride, we'll figure something else out."

"Yeah, but what about evenings I don't work? Should I just be a prisoner at night?"

"Your place is warded, isn't it?"

I couldn't help but glance at the bar's front door. "Oh, yeah. No one is getting in there. But if I can't go out, I might as well be in jail. That's no way to live."

I was going stir crazy sitting in that apartment alone. I went out for a run in the mornings when I woke up, and I came to work, then I went home to sleep, and it all started over again. If I couldn't go out at all, I knew I'd go berserk. Lizzy's brunch group was the only social life I had, and in spite of being skeptical about it at first, I found myself looking forward to it.

As I worked, I noticed Sam circulating around the bar, stopping and talking to various people. He also had a long conversation with Blair before the policeman left. Then Sam came over and explained the plan.

"Are you sure?" I asked.

"Carleton knew not to mess with Rosie's," Sam said. "If I have to educate a new generation, then so be it."

---

I was almost at the bus stop when a dozen vampires appeared as if by magic. Their speed always gave them an advantage when dealing with humans or shifters. I recognized a few of them from the previous night.

"Back for more?" I asked, casting a personal shield to protect myself.

"You think you're smart," one of them said, immediately lowering my already low opinion of his intelligence.

He snarled, showing his fangs, and leapt toward me. A gun fired to my right and behind me, and a small explosion left a large hole in the vampire's chest. He crashed to the ground, and his clothing caught on fire.

A fireball whooshed by me on my left, and another vamp turned into a torch. He let out a high, keening sound.

Several of the vampires had already started toward me, and their momentum carried them forward. Some of the others milled around in apparent confusion.

I sent a burst of force toward the three who were closest to me, and they stumbled backward. Another gunshot knocked one of them down, and he, too, caught on fire. A bolt of lightning hit another one, and the air seemed to open above the third, pouring water over her, and then the water froze solid, anchoring her in place. I turned to see who might have pulled that trick, and saw Sam was the closest person to her. I hadn't known he was an aeromancer.

Before I could think about the wisdom of what I was doing, I jumped forward, and grabbed two of the vampires, one by the hair and one by the throat. I slammed their heads together, three times, then booted the guy in the gut, sending him flying away. A girl swung at me and I blocked the blow, then punched her in the face, burying my fist halfway into her skull.

A flare of fire and light was accompanied by more keening, and I saw a second vampire turn into a torch.

More fireballs came from other directions, with predictable results. The gun fired again, and a woman landed on the ground next to me, shock in her face and her clothing erupting in flame. She opened her mouth in a scream, but with her lungs blown away, no sound came out.

Two more guns fired from farther away, and two more vamps went down.

Someone shouted, "Freeze! Hands in the air!"

I saw the vampires still standing hold their hands in the air. Several men, some in police uniforms, ran out of the darkness, pointing pistols at the vampires' heads and ordering them to lie on the ground. Once the vampires lay down, the men clamped heavy shackles on their wrists and ankles.

Someone approached me, and before I could strike, I realized it was Blair, with a large pistol in his hand.

I nodded to the pistol. "Very impressive. What kind of ammunition are you using?"

"High-explosive incendiaries. It doesn't kill them, but it disables them for a while. The more they burn, the longer it takes for them to recover."

"Shoot them in the head if you want to kill them," I said. "The reason people cut their heads off is to separate the brain from the body. If their brains are scattered to kingdom come, they can't regenerate."

"I thought you didn't know anything about vampires," he said.

I gave him a smile. "Did you know that gnomes are primarily insectivores, although they do like a bit of greens with their bugs. They're particularly fond of lambs quarter and chickweed, though they also like purslane, pigweed, and a number of other common weeds. They don't seem to like flowers and vegetables, though. That's why they're called garden gnomes."

He stared at me with his mouth hanging open.

Looking around at a number of men and women I had never seen before who were taking charge of the vampires, I said, "Thank you, Lieutenant. I'm pleasantly surprised. When Sam told me the two of you wanted to set up an ambush, I was rather dubious. This worked far better than I ever dreamed."

He looked down at the girl with the caved-in face lying in a pool of blood, then looked back up at me.

"That's pretty impressive, too."

I shrugged. "Magic, Lieutenant. And a black belt. Not as flashy as fireballs and lightning bolts, but I make do with what I have."

Not that I wouldn't love the ability to throw fireballs and shoot lightning bolts. And that trick Sam pulled with the water was pretty cool, too. My magic was solely tied to the ley lines. I pulled the power and redirected it, but I couldn't transform it. I did know a few witch spells, but that was another story.

Sam gave me a ride home, and I discovered that Josh and Trevor were the mages throwing fireballs and lightning bolts. I wondered if I had been a little too rough on them. When he dropped me off, I thought about what having friends would mean. Obviously, it meant sticking up for them if they had troubles and feeling free to ask for help to solve your own problems.

That was a strange concept. As a Hunter, if I had to ask for help, it was marked down as a failure, a sign that I was inadequate. Looking around my empty apartment, I felt rather inadequate to deal with my new world.

## CHAPTER 9

L iam was behind the bar and Blair was sitting at the bar drinking coffee when I walked in the next afternoon.

"Hello, Liam," I said. He turned to look at me and dipped his head in acknowledgement, then went back to staring at the room. He had never acknowledged such a greeting before, and I was so shocked I almost dropped my coat. I hung it up and said, "Good afternoon, Lieutenant. Just coffee today, or are you planning on dinner?"

"Maybe later. I need you to come down to my office and give a statement concerning last night and the incident the previous night."

"Can't I do it here?"

He shook his head. "It needs to be a formal statement on the record. We have enough to hold the prisoners we took, but to put them away, we need your testimony as the victim of their crimes."

"And as soon as they heal and bond out, I'll have to deal with them again."

I was attracting entirely too much attention from Blair and the police. Sooner or later, he or someone he worked with would decide to check on my background and find out I didn't have one. Other than abruptly disappearing while in middle school, then abruptly reappearing to file for a passport five years later, I didn't exist. I could come up with a story about living in a cult or a hippie commune, but putting together an air-tight background would take some time and careful thought.

Then there was the possibility, slim I thought, that I had left a fingerprint or DNA sample at one of the murders I committed for the Illuminati. I hoped there wasn't any evidence in anyone's database tying me to a crime, but I couldn't be completely sure. I was trained not to make assumptions. "The wrong assumption will get you killed," Master Robyn had said more than once. "If it's not a verifiable fact, you can't rely on it."

I went back to Sam's office and spoke to him, and he encouraged me to cooperate with the police. With a sigh, I went back to the bar.

"All right. When?" I asked Blair.

"Tomorrow? Set a time and I'll make the arrangements." He handed me his card. I looked at the address and had no idea where it was but figured I could use my map to find a bus route to take me there.

"Do you like working here?" Blair asked, taking me by surprise.

"Yeah, I do. The people are nice and Sam's a good boss. Some people say they care about their employees, but how many people would do what he did for me last night?" I shrugged. "There are always assholes you have to put up with working in a bar, but this place is better than most." Hell, it was my dream job. I had expected to end up working as a hotel maid cleaning toilets or something.

"Where did you go to school?" That was a question I didn't expect.

"Nowhere."

He looked surprised. "You never went to college?"

I laughed. "I never graduated from high school. I'm a dropout, Lieutenant." I certainly wasn't going to tell him about the education I had received. He wouldn't have believed it anyway. "Why?"

Blair shrugged. "I'm always looking for good people that can help me out."

A job? "Do the police hire high school dropouts?"

He shook his head and stared down at his coffee cup. "No, we don't." Looking up at me, he said, "I do contract consulting services from people in the paranormal community, though. If you'd like to make some extra money."

I laughed again. "We're a community?" I immediately thought about how nice it would be to have a chair for my apartment. "Extra money is always nice. What kind of consulting do you think I could do?"

"It depends on what your talents are."

"Oh." I took an involuntary step back. Telling Blair, or anyone else, about my abilities wasn't something I was prepared to do—then or anytime in the far foreseeable future. 'Yes, Lieutenant, I'm a trained assassin, seductress, and fighter.' That would go over well. All my training involved either attack or defense or spying. I wasn't even sure how marketable any of them would be for any organization except maybe the CIA or another shadowy secret cult such as the Illuminati. And that wasn't something I ever wanted to get involved with again, to be a pawn for powerful men seeking to gather more power and wealth. I couldn't imagine ever trusting anyone playing such games.

"I don't think I have anything useful," I said. "Not like those guys with *Lost and Found*, or one of the seers."

"Why don't you tell me what you can do and let me figure it out," he said.

I took a deep breath. "Do you know the difference between a witch and a mage?"

"Not…really."

"A witch pulls on energy from the world around her and uses some sort of ritual or spell to twist reality. Some may pull their energy from the earth or plants or animals, or even from something like an electrical line. They study and experiment and learn how to use that energy to cast their spells. With me so far?"

"Yeah. I think so."

"Okay. There are other energy sources that run throughout the earth called ley lines, and that is where mages get their power. Depending on how far a mage is from a line, and how powerful the line is, determines how much power he can pull from the line and use. Think of them like rivers and streams of raw magic of varying sizes. Mages tend to have an affinity for a particular type of magic. A mage twists ley energy into a physical manifestation. Like last night with the fireballs and lightning bolts. We call that pyromancy and electrokinesis."

"Got it."

"I can't do any of that. I'm what's called a ley line mage. All I can do is pull ley line energy and redirect it. I don't convert it."

His face showed his confusion as he tried to figure out what I was saying. "I'm not sure I understand."

"I know." I wasn't about to explain all the ways I was able to twist and manipulate ley line energy, but I would probably be of more use to a construction or mining company than to the police.

A customer came up to the bar, and I moved away to take his order.

The City of the Illuminati sat on the intersection of two very powerful ley lines. That was the energy Strickland used to destroy the City of the Illuminati, using the crystal as a focus. My new home of Westport sat between two powerful ley lines that intersected east of the city. That was one of the things that drew me there, and that accounted for the large number of paranormals who gathered in that area. A minor ley line ran beneath Rosie's and on toward the port, directly under my apartment complex as well. I didn't have to ask why Eleanor built the apartments where she did.

Blair eventually ordered dinner, and when he paid his tab, he asked, "So, you'll come by tomorrow?"

"Yeah. One o'clock okay?"

"That will work."

Later that evening, the three mouseketeers came in and took a table near the pool tables. Jenny took their order and came to the bar.

"I'll take care of them," I told her. "I want to thank them for last night."

She smiled and nodded, then headed back to the kitchen.

I took their drinks out to them and said, "On me, and thanks for last night."

Josh looked almost shocked, the other two showed mild surprise.

"You're more than welcome," Trevor said, raising his glass to me. "It was fun."

I raised an eyebrow. "You have a strange definition of fun," I said, and he grinned.

"Yeah, not a problem. Thanks for the drink," Josh said.

Jolene smiled. "I just watched. I let the boys do all the flashy stuff. But it didn't look as though you needed much help."

I smiled back at her. "Maybe, but I'm not super woman, and there were a lot of them."

"You should have taken a weapon," Josh said, motioning to the tray I held.

I laughed and went back behind the bar.

———

The following day, I took the bus downtown, and it dropped me off right at the police station. But that wasn't the address on Blair's business card. After asking a policeman, I walked three blocks to the District Court building. I couldn't find anything about the PCU on the building directory, but I remembered Sam telling me that Blair reported to the District Attorney, so I went to that office.

"I'm a little lost," I told the receptionist. "I'm looking for Lieutenant Blair."

"Oh, yes. Go out to the corridor, take a right, and then take the back stairs down to the basement. When you get there, walk down the corridor, then take the second corridor to the right. His office is about halfway down, just before you get to the bathrooms."

So, that's what I did. The basement was dingy, and about half-lighted. When I finally found an office that said, "P. Crimes" painted on the glass of the door, I was next to the restrooms, and beyond them were two large metal doors spanning the breadth of the hallway with a sign that said, "Loading Dock." Obviously, Blair hung out in the high-rent district.

I tried the door, but it was locked, so I pushed what looked to be a doorbell. Then waited. After a while, I pushed the button again. As I started to turn away, a voice from a speaker next to the button said, "Yes?"

"I have an appointment with Lieutenant Blair."

"Your name?"

"Erin McLane."

"Just a moment."

I stood there for another few minutes, then a buzz came from the door. When I tried the handle again, the door swung open.

Inside, the office was better lit than the hallway, but still as dingy. A woman in her thirties with orange hair stood behind a counter, and beyond her, I saw a number of cubicles.

"Come with me, please," the woman said, and without looking back took off down a narrow hallway. I followed her past the cubicles on one side and several doors on the other side until we reached a door at the end.

"Go on in," she said, turning around and going back in the direction we came from.

I turned the knob and walked into the office beyond. Blair had his jacket off and sat behind a desk piled high with precarious-looking stacks of paper and manila folders.

He glanced up, and said, "Please sit down, Ms. McLane. I'll be with you in just a minute."

I sat for five minutes while he typed on the computer and then, finally, pushed the keyboard away.

"Sorry to keep you waiting." He stood, walked around the desk, and opened the door. "We'll be doing this in one of the interview rooms."

I followed him out, and at the end of the corridor, he took a left into the cubicles. Some of them were obviously unoccupied, others had computers and papers on the desks, and a couple of them actually had people. We passed a cube where the woman with the orange hair sat, and then stopped at another cube.

"Frankie, Ms. McLane is here," Blair said. Then to me, "Frankie Jones is one of my colleagues. She'll be sitting in on your interview."

Frankie turned out to be a stunning black woman who was at least six feet tall. I would have judged her to be in her early thirties, but the symbols of witchcraft hanging on the walls of her cube made me defer that assumption. Telling the ages of paranormals was always tricky.

Blair led me back to one of the doors opposite the cubes that I had seen earlier. Inside was a table, four chairs, and a camera on the wall.

"Is this where you interrogate your prisoners?" I asked.

"This is it," Frankie said with a smile. She winked at me. "We keep the torture devices behind a hidden door."

She laid what looked like a Native American

dreamcatcher on the table in front of her. There was a tape recorder on the table. We sat down, and Blair turned it on, then he asked me to tell them about the night Lizzy intervened with the vampires. I wasn't sure who else they had talked to, so I tried to give as sparse an account as I could but kept with the truth. Next, they asked me to tell them about the ambush Blair and Sam set up the night before.

When I finished, Frankie asked me several questions that were mostly aimed at why I felt threatened and why the vampires accosted me. Blair hadn't said a word through the entire interview.

"You're a ley line mage, is that correct?" Frankie asked. To that point, magic hadn't been mentioned.

I pointedly looked at the tape recorder and then back to her. Blair leaned forward and turned off the recorder. I glanced up at the camera and pushed some magic at it. They wouldn't find out it was broken until they tried to play the recording of my interview.

"Yes, that's correct," I said. "I don't know what that has to do with anything."

She shifted her questions again. "Are you aware of a Hunter here in the city?"

"No, I'm not. I know a lot of people have speculated about one, but I haven't seen one, or any evidence of one."

"Are you aware that several vampires have been decapitated recently?"

"So I've been told."

"If not a Hunter, who do you suppose might be responsible for that?"

"I don't know."

"What do you know about the Illuminati?"

Now, that was something I didn't expect. "Weren't they one of those secret societies like the Freemasons and the Rosicrucians?"

"Why did you come to Westport?"

"I flew in on my broomstick because I heard the weather was balmy and I hoped to improve my tan," I said. It was the most outrageous lie I could think of off the top of my head, considering the temperature outside was in the forties and it had been overcast for days. Frankie nodded, then her eyes widened, and she stared at me. "And if you think that truth spell is going to catch me in a lie, you're sadly mistaken, Ms. Jones." I turned to Blair. "Are we through?"

He gave me a tight smile. "Yes, thank you." He and Frankie exchanged a look I couldn't decipher.

Maybe I shouldn't have been so blunt, but I was getting tired, and the whole interview irritated the hell out of me. Either I was going to tell them the truth or I was going to lie my ass off, and trying to trick me with their line of questioning wasn't going to change that. They already knew I was a mage. Did they think I was so ignorant that I didn't know a lie catcher when I saw one?

When we stood, Blair said, "I hope you'll reconsider signing on as a consultant. I think you could really help us out."

"If you come up with a specific task you think I can help with, let me know, and I'll consider it," I said. "And Ms. Jones, come by Rosie's sometime. I think you'd like it. Bring the other witch I met earlier with you."

# CHAPTER 10

That night was one of my nights off work, and Lizzy had invited me to go out clubbing with her.

"Come with me," she pleaded. "We'll go dancing and it will be fun."

I wasn't sure about that. The only dancing I had ever done was ballroom dancing. It was part of my training aimed at getting close to powerful old men the Illuminati targeted. But I agreed to go. Sitting around my empty apartment by myself was starting to get really boring. I had gone to a used book store and bought a few dog-eared paperbacks, but I had read them all.

I took the bus, and then walked to a café downtown that Lizzy liked. After dinner, we strolled down by the ocean, something I still hadn't seen since coming to town. I thought about how strange that was. I had my days off, and I had always enjoyed walks out in nature but totally missed that opportunity in Westport.

A cold wind blew in, but I faced into it and breathed deeply. The air smelled clean and fresh. After a few minutes, I realized Lizzy was shivering and her teeth were chattering.

"Hey, are you cold? I'm sorry." I pulled her into a hug and drew on the nearest ley line to generate some heat as we walked back to where we were sheltered from the wind by tall buildings.

Lizzy was dressed in all her emo glory—pink top, floral pink miniskirt that barely covered her butt, horizontally striped pink-and-white tights—and I worried that my white top and new blue jeans would be too sedate. The nightclub was exactly what I feared—loud, garish, and crowded. But Lizzy came alive in that setting. Her face lit up, and she laughed at everything. Considering her preferred drink was fairly low in alcohol, I didn't worry about her getting hammered. I had never seen her truly drunk at Rosie's except the night people were buying us drinks.

I stuck with beer and a self-imposed limit of three.

Lizzy knew a lot of the people, and we had barely taken a sip of our first drink when a guy asked her to dance. She asked me to hold her drink, and I told her I would look for a table.

"Erin!" someone shouted as I wandered around the bar.

It took me a minute to figure out who was calling out to me, and then I saw Trevor standing and waving at me. I made my way across the room and found Josh and Jolene sitting at the table with Trevor.

"I never would have guessed you were a two-fisted drinker," Josh said.

"It's Lizzy's," I said with a laugh and took a seat between Jolene and Trevor.

"The pink popsicle?" Josh asked.

I leaned close to Jolene, who was taking a sip of her drink. "You would think by his age he might have figured out why he's never had a date."

She snorted, spraying the table, and started coughing. When she recovered, she shot me a glance and winked.

"So, what have you been doing with your day off?" Trevor asked.

"Undergoing the inquisition at Lieutenant Blair's office."

"Ah, yes. We did that this morning," he said. "Didn't take too long."

"Really? I was there for two hours. Blair and some witch who works with him named Frankie grilled me on everything they could think of."

"Frankie?" Jolene asked.

"Yeah. He introduced her as Frankie Jones."

The rolled eyes of all three tipped me off that something wasn't quite right.

"Tall black lady?" Jolene asked. I nodded. She put her hand on my arm. "That was Francis Jones, Assistant District Attorney. Blair's boss. And she's not a witch, she's a mage. An aeromancer."

I stared at her. "She was in a cube with lots of witchy stuff, and she brought a lie catcher into the interview."

"Window dressing," Trevor said. "Distraction. That was someone else's cube. Girl, you got the big gun pointed at you. What kind of questions did they ask you?"

Shaking my head, I said, "All kinds of stuff about Hunters and the Illuminati, and a bunch of other fanciful bullshit. For some reason, Blair and the vamps seem to think I'm a big, bad Hunter. But no one has explained how I managed to decapitate a bunch of people before I even got to town."

"Magic," Jolene said, and everyone burst out laughing.

Lizzy found us and sat down, then Trevor asked me to dance. I must have looked somewhat panicked, because Jolene and Lizzy teased me into going with him. I discovered it wasn't very difficult. I watched the other women and just shook my butt and waved my hands in time to the music. Trevor didn't seem embarrassed to be dancing with me, so I decided it was good enough.

"Where did you live before you came to Westport?" Jolene asked.

The kind of question I dreaded, but I had been asked about my past several times at the bar. I gave her the standard answer I had devised.

"I really don't like to talk about the past. I'm here, I'm starting over, and I only want to think about the future," I said. I knew of some of the rumors concerning me at the bar. People speculated that I was running from an abusive relationship. Lizzy told Jenny that she thought I had escaped from a cult. Not too far off the truth.

During the course of the evening I discovered that Jolene was a finder-tracker and Josh's older sister. Trevor was an electrokinetic and a computer whiz, and Josh was a pyromancer and the brawn of their group.

I tried to relax, but the only times in my life when I'd been in social situations I was on a mission, and old habits were hard to break. I found myself memorizing the faces of everyone who came within ten feet of our table, and by the end of the evening, I knew the body language—every expression and gesture—of the people sitting with me.

Josh drank heavily, just as he did when he came into Rosie's, and got louder and more obnoxious as the evening wore on. The louder he got, the quieter Jolene got and the more Trevor tried to talk to me and divert my attention. I had danced with Josh a couple of times, and he kept his hands to himself, but his leering and fixation on my chest made me uncomfortable. Trevor, on the other hand, always smiled at me, and when he ran his eyes up and down, it gave me kind of a warm feeling.

Josh suddenly leaned across the table and said, "You're really, really pretty, and you've got a great body. Why don't you like me?"

It took me a moment to find my voice. "Because you're loud, obnoxious, and rude, and you get worse the more you drink."

He fell back in his chair. "Shit. I'm hot, you know."

"Not every girl wants to combust."

Lizzy giggled, and Jolene looked down at her lap, her hair falling forward and hiding her face, her shoulders shaking. I thought I detected strange squeaking noises.

It got late and Lizzy called a cab. I begged off, telling her I would take the bus. I still hadn't received my first paycheck and was living off my tips and my shift meal at the bar.

As I rose to go outside with Lizzy, Trevor leaned close and said, "I would enjoy taking you out to dinner sometime. Maybe a movie?" He slipped me a bar napkin with his name and a phone number.

"Maybe," I replied. He wasn't much taller than I

was, so it was easy to meet his eyes. He was very handsome and nice, and I found myself wanting to say yes. "I work most evenings."

"I know your schedule."

I put the napkin in the pocket of my coat and bid everyone good night, then walked outside with Lizzy.

"Did you have fun?" she asked as we stood outside the club.

"Yeah, I did. Thanks for inviting me."

"Trevor likes you. He's so dreamy, and he really is a nice guy."

"Why don't you have a boyfriend?" I asked. "Maybe Trevor?"

She shook her head. "Trevor and I dated for a year in college, but he's a little too vanilla for me. I think the two of you would fit nicely, though. As to most guys, I scare them," she said. "Guys get kinda weird when they find out I'm smarter than they are. And the nerds I meet at school don't turn me on at all. Are you going to be all right? Women normally don't walk alone this late at night."

"If someone hassles me, I'll tell them to back off because I know the girl in the pink car."

She laughed. Her taxi came, and I waved to her as it drove off.

It was four blocks to the bus stop, and as I walked through the drizzle, I calculated if I could spare the money to buy an umbrella. Since I didn't have one, I threw up a small shield over my head. I justified it to myself because it was dark, late at night, and very few people were on the street.

Walking past an alley, I heard a noise. I stopped and peered into the darkness. A bar of faint light illuminated a figure dressed all in black, balaclava covering its head. I immediately shielded myself. It turned to me, then gathered itself and leaped to the top of a building. It looked back at me once, then disappeared.

I had discovered the Hunter. I immediately shielded, and my first impulse was to head in the other direction as quickly as possible.

Bracing myself, I made my way down the alley, where I found a vampire with his head lying several feet away from his body. I could understand the shocked look on his face. I had seen it before when I decapitated a creature who thought he was invincible and immortal.

But what captured my attention was the young girl wearing a red minidress, probably around my age, who was lying a little farther away. Her dress was pulled up around her waist, and her bloody panties were ripped to shreds. Her throat was savaged, not a neat, simple bite. The vampire had no intention to leave her alive, feeding as he raped her.

I checked her pulse just in case, but she was dead.

I stood over her, feeling helpless. She, and others like her, was the reason I had embraced my role as a Hunter. There wasn't any room for ambiguity, no debate about right or wrong. If I had come along before the Hunter did, I would have killed the vampire myself.

Without a phone, I didn't know what to do. I left the alley and looked around for a pay phone, but those had become rare over the past few years. I struggled with myself, on the one hand, knowing there wasn't anything I could do to help her, and on the other hand, not wanting to leave her in that filthy alley for the rats.

In the end, I walked back to the club to call the cops. I found Blair's card in my pocket and gave it to the bouncer. "Can you please call this number? There's a girl in an alley."

I don't know what he saw when he looked at my face, but he didn't ask me any questions and made the call.

A few minutes later, a dark car pulled up in front of the club. The orange-haired witch I had seen at Blair's office and a tall, dark-haired man got out and approached me where I stood with the bouncer.

"Ms. McLane?" the witch asked, showing her badge and ID to me and the bouncer.

"Yes."

"Are you the one who called us?"

"Yes. It's a couple of blocks from here. Between here and the bus stop."

"Why don't you get in and you can direct us."

So, I did.

"I'm detective Mackle," the woman said as she put the car in gear. "This is detective sergeant Bailey. Which direction?" I could tell that Bailey was a mage.

When we got there, we walked down the alley—the cops with pistols in one hand and flashlights in the other. A couple of inquisitive rats ran from the lights, but otherwise, the scene was just as I had left it.

"Oh, Jesus," Mackle said when her light fell on the girl. She turned away and threw up. I had to admit, it looked a lot worse in the light.

Bailey was on his phone, and he sent Mackle back to their car. She strung that yellow crime-scene tape across the alley entrance, and then came back, handing him a pair of rubber gloves and some covers that he slipped over his shoes.

"Ms. McLane, if you'll come with me," she said, motioning back to their car.

I was glad to comply. The dead vamp didn't bother me, but my stomach wanted to rebel every time I looked at the girl. It didn't take a genius to figure out she had been walking to my bus stop from either the club I was at or one of the others in the neighborhood. Her bad luck was that she had left the bar before I did. I almost felt guilty the vamp hadn't found me first.

"Are you all right?" Mackle asked.

"Yeah. Are you?" She still looked a little pale.

In answer, she said, "I see a lot of ugly things on this job, but that took me by surprise." She shook her head. "Why did the vampire have to do that?"

"Rage," I said, and shrugged. "He was punishing her, or maybe all women, or maybe he just had a bad day at the office and she happened to land in his sights."

She cocked her head to look at me for a long moment, then said, "Why don't you tell me what you saw."

So, I told her. And when Blair and the forensics team showed up, I told Blair. And when Frankie Jones showed up, I told it all again.

"You think it was a Hunter," Jones said when I finished.

"It was a Hunter. Don't ask me how or why I know. I haven't lied to you yet, except about the broomstick, so don't make me start."

Her eyes widened, and then she nodded. "Fair enough."

"I really flew in on a mop." I don't know what prompted me to say that, but it got a startled bark of laughter from her before she sobered again.

Jones drove me home around four o'clock, and I was dead tired. When I got out of the car, I leaned back in and said, "Ms. Jones, I'm on your side. All I want to do is live my life in peace. I don't have anything against vampires, or werewolves, or anything else that goes bump in the night as long as it leaves me alone. But until an old vamp manages to establish dominance in this city, things are going to get worse, not better. Fasten your seatbelt. You're in for a wild ride."

## CHAPTER 11

I woke up far past my usual waking time. A look at what I had in the fridge and the cupboard helped me decide to blow off my morning run. Instead, I took a shower and caught the bus down to Rosie's.

I had borrowed Sam's computer and his credit card to buy a monthly bus pass, which cut a significant amount off my transportation costs and gave me more freedom to explore the city. But that morning I had a specific menu selection I wanted to try.

Sam raised an eyebrow when I walked in and plunked myself on a barstool.

"A full Irish with coffee," I said. A full Irish breakfast totaled about fourteen hundred calories, and I looked forward to enjoying every one of them.

"That will destroy your slender girlish figure," he said as he poured my coffee. "Take care, Lassie, or you'll end up looking like me." He grinned and patted his stomach.

"I'd have to order it a lot more often," I said,

grinning back, "but I'll take your warning under consideration."

I took a sip of my coffee, then said, "I had a rather unsettling experience last night," and went on to tell him of my encounter with the Hunter and the dead girl.

"You're sure it was a Hunter," he asked, "and not some other kind of ninja wannabe?"

One of the kitchen staff came out with my breakfast. An egg, Irish bacon, sausage, baked beans, fried potatoes, black pudding, white pudding, and half of a grilled tomato. When the girl had gone, I said, "Yes, I'm sure. I've seen a Hunter before."

That got me a raised eyebrow. "You said it, and you said he."

"Yeah. I wasn't sure at first, but the more I think about it, size—height and bulk—make me think it was a man. Sam, he jumped to the top of a roof, at least twelve feet up, as easily as someone might jump up on this bar."

He chuckled, holding his stomach. "Easy for you to say. I doubt I could climb onto this bar."

"Sam, I told Frankie last night that a Hunter wouldn't be here just to take out a few rogue vampires. There's a reason he's here, and with the Master of the City gone, things will be chaotic until a new Master appears and establishes control. But the Hunter would know that, so why did he take out Carleton? There's something else going on."

"You seem to know a lot about Hunters."

"I read a lot, and I once had access to an arcane book on Hunters and the Illuminati."

He chuckled again. "The Illuminati? I thought that was an old myth."

"Frankie Jones doesn't think so. She asked me what I knew about them when I gave my statement yesterday."

That drew a long look. "Interesting."

"I thought so. Sam, how many high-ranking people in this city are paranormals?"

"A lot. Jones and her boss, the DA, at least one member of the City Council, and a state senator. There's also a shifter on the Council. The head of one of the largest corporations headquartered here is a mage, and Carleton owned the company that hauls the garbage. That's one of the reasons trash pickup is at night. And the Catholic bishop here is a witch. A white witch, but a witch just the same."

Well, that put a number of things in perspective. With the City of the Illuminati gone, along with the entire ruling Council, those Illuminati out in the world who had infiltrated government, industries, and churches were suddenly on their own. I knew for a fact that few of them knew each other. The Council kept a tight rein on their subordinates, and while the station chiefs in London, Munich, and Cuzco had more knowledge and understanding of the organization's strategies and goals than the average member, no one had the whole picture. Two members of the Order might know each other for years without knowing the other was part of the Order.

But when directives stopped coming from the City, highly placed insurgents would take whatever measures they felt necessary to enhance their own and the Order's goals. And since the major goals were power and wealth, that was what they would pursue.

Calling in a Hunter, or multiple Hunters, to facilitate an ascent in position would be a logical action.

"Is something wrong with your breakfast?" Sam asked.

"No. Why?"

"You stopped eating."

I realized I had a forkful of egg and sausage halfway to my mouth. I shook myself out of my reverie and chomped the mouthful.

When I finished chewing, I asked, "Do you have any contacts in DC or New York?"

He shook his head. "Why?"

"You said there had been a rash of beheadings in other cities." If my guess was correct and the Illuminati were making a push, there were more of them in New York and Washington than anywhere else on the continent.

"This book you mentioned."

"Yes?" I suddenly wondered if I'd said too much.

"You think it was true?"

"The person who wrote it thought it was true, and the person who gave it to me certainly did."

He nodded, seeming to drift off into thought.

---

From Rosie's I went to the public library and went through the hassle of getting a library card without a driver's license. Luckily, I had my rental agreement, and with that and my passport, they finally decided I was entitled to borrow their books.

What I did was reserve time on a computer, which was in a tiny cubicle with a huge red sign admonishing me that I was not allowed to access any porn sites, and also telling me that such sites were blocked and I couldn't see them anyway.

Looking up the DA and Frankie and the bishop was pretty straightforward. I wasn't sure what I was trying to find but hoped that some pieces of information might help to identify a thread that would lead me to a network of mages who controlled Westport. The bishop didn't worry me since the Illuminati were all mages. But I read everything I could find about him, thinking that in a pinch he might be an ally. I chuckled when I discovered that his sister ran a tea shop advertising herbs and "natural remedies."

Frankie turned out to be the daughter of the DA's former law partner and had gone to his university. From the DA's Wikipedia page, I followed threads of information through the organizations he belonged to. One of those was a private club, the membership of which was secret. But a Google search turned up twenty more influential individuals, all in the Westport area, who claimed membership in that club.

Little information was available on The Columbia Club, but comparing public information about its members was enlightening. The members included a Westport city councilman, a state senator, and at least two of the members who might be classified as heads "of one of the largest corporations headquartered here." Frankie's father was also a member, as was the mayor's chief of staff. It appeared that paranormals had an inordinate amount of influence in the city.

Pairing that with a shifter on the City Council and Carleton's waste disposal business, I wondered how they managed to keep the conspiracy theorists from going bananas. But somehow Blair and his bosses managed to keep it all quiet. Actually, I thought, that might have been the true purpose of Blair's unit.

———

From the library, I hiked a mile to the building where the Columbia Club's address was listed. I found a private mailbox company, and when I enquired about getting a box, the guy at the counter assured me of absolute confidentiality and that my address would appear as a real address, not a mailbox. That left me with nothing, since I couldn't find an online presence for the club. No web page, no announcements of meetings, no charitable activities.

I found a pay phone in the lobby of a chain restaurant, and pulling Trevor's number out of my pocket, I gave him a call.

"Trevor," he answered.

"Hi. This is Erin."

"Oh, wow. Hi, how are you doing?"

"Okay. Hey, Jolene mentioned that you're a computer whiz."

He laughed. "I do okay. What's up?"

"I need to find out about a group, a private club, and I can't find anything about them online. I was hoping you could help me."

"Possibly. Are you sure they have an online presence?"

"I'm thinking they might not. Could I come over and talk to you about it?"

"Sure." He sounded eager, and I felt a little guilty if he thought I was interested in dating him. At least I didn't think I was interested, but I got a warm, happy feeling when I thought about him. He gave me his address, and I pulled out my map of the city.

The distance between Trevor's house and Rosie's surprised me. He lived in a suburb south of the city near the coast, and Rosie's was on the west side. It took me over an hour to get from the library downtown to his place by bus.

The bus dropped me off at a train station, and I walked three blocks to his house, a small rancher among similar houses with neatly trimmed front lawns and flowered borders. Many had children's toys on the front lawns or basketball hoops hanging over the garages. It vaguely reminded me of the neighborhood where I had lived with my parents.

Trevor was dressed in a t-shirt and jeans when he answered the doorbell. He opened the screen door, and I saw that he was barefoot and his hair was damp.

"Come in," he said with a smile. "This is a pleasant surprise."

"Well, as I told you on the phone, I'm trying to find out something about a particular group, and I'm striking out. Jolene told me that her magic involves finding and tracking, but you're the cyber expert on the team."

"Jolene was being modest. She does okay with computers. So, what is this group?"

"It's called the Columbia Club. I discovered its existence because a number of paranormals in high positions here in Westport listed membership in it, along with various civic and charitable organizations. But when I tried to look it up, I came up blank."

"Come on back." He led me to a bedroom filled with computer equipment instead of a bed. I wasn't sure what computers cost, but I recognized that he must have had tens of thousands of dollars invested. For the first time I realized that Lost and Found was a real business. And I was asking him to help me for free.

He sat down at a keyboard, and three monitors came to life. "So, the Columbia Club? And it's kind of a private organization?"

All my adult life, I had gotten what I wanted by manipulating people, even Master Benedict and the heads of the Hunters' Guild. The people I had met at Rosie's offered me friendship openly, asking nothing in return. Some had even put their lives on the line for me. All Sam asked was honesty. I suddenly realized that since I was a child, I had never had a friend, had no idea how to be one. Wasn't even sure what the word meant except in an abstract sense.

I shook my head. "I'm sorry. This is how you make your living. I thought I'd just come over and flirt with you a little and get something for free. But that's not how people treat their friends, is it? I'll go."

Whirling about, I headed for the door, tears half blinding me, and not understanding the feelings that suddenly washed over me.

Trevor caught me halfway across the living room, laying a hand on my shoulder and turning me around.

"Hey. What's wrong?"

I felt ashamed and refused to meet his eyes. Then I blurted, "Everyone has been so nice to me, and I've just been a stone-cold bitch, afraid to let anyone get close to me."

My mind froze. I couldn't believe I had said that out loud. I tried to pull away from him, but instead found myself pulled into a hug, pressed against him. He was warm, and solid, and felt safe. I didn't know what to do, my arms hanging at my sides. I was afraid to return the hug. The only time I had ever hugged someone was during sex.

"You haven't been a bitch," he said, "except maybe to Josh, and he deserved it. You're sweet and funny, and nice."

"You're lying to make me feel better."

"A little bit, maybe."

I looked up into his face and saw a soft smile and kind eyes.

"That's what friends do," Trevor said, "try to make you feel better. Now, come back and tell me why we're concerned about the Columbia Club, okay?" He shrugged. "I've been paid a lot less than with a little harmless flirting."

We went back into the computer room, and he pulled a chair up so I could watch what he did.

"Now, tell me what we're looking for."

I started by telling him about the Hunter and the vampire and the dead girl. "The thing is," I said, "I've read a lot about Hunters, and they don't just wander around killing vampires. Someone called him here for a reason."

Trevor nodded. "And you think this Columbia Club might be the ones who contracted him."

"Not the club itself, but one or two of its members. I think someone is making a power play, and those in the club are likely targets. Think about it. In any society, most of the money and power is held by a very small group. Now, if an even smaller group of paranormals was pulling the strings behind the scene, they could get almost anything they wanted."

His eyes widened slightly at that. Based on my

answers to his questions, he began a number of searches, turning up references across the country to people killed by beheading in the previous few weeks. He also cross-referenced other powerful and influential men all over North America who were connected to the Columbia Club members in one way or another.

Then he called up a program I'd never seen before and began searches using it, based on a number of keywords from our conversation.

"What is that?" I asked.

"It's sometimes called the Dark Web," he answered. "The underbelly of the internet that's encrypted and carries traffic and information people don't want the world, especially law enforcement, to see. You know, things like child pornography, criminal conspiracies, hacker websites with stolen data to sell, that sort of thing. Spies and secret societies like the Illuminati and the Ku Klux Klan use it, as well as drug dealers and arms merchants. If your Columbia Club members are communicating electronically, this is where they might go."

"The Illuminati?"

"Yeah. A bunch of conspiracy nuts who have plans for taking over the world. There are a bunch of groups like that playing on the Dark Web."

"Can you actually get into those kinds of sites, like the Illuminati?"

Trevor shook his head. "I can see them, but usually you have to have a key of some sort to get in. You know, like a password. That Illuminati site isn't even in English. It's like some kind of made-up language that looks a little like German but isn't."

He spent some time writing several short programs,

then said, "It might take some time for these searches to run. If you have time tomorrow afternoon, we can look at the results then."

"Sure, I can do that. Thanks."

He looked at his watch. "Are you hungry? Want to go get a pizza and I'll walk you to the train station?"

"Okay. I didn't take the train, though."

"You came by bus? That must have taken forever. Do you have a transit pass?"

"Yeah."

"There's a train station one bus stop past your apartment. You can take the train from here to downtown, then switch to the train out to the west side. It takes me about half an hour, maybe forty minutes, to get to Rosie's from here."

When we got outside, I asked, "How far are we from the ocean here?"

"From the bay? About three blocks."

"Bay, ocean—what's the difference? It's all the same thing, isn't it?"

He laughed. "I guess so. Want to go see?"

We walked down the street until it ended in a park, then we followed a path that ended in a waist-high wall. A break in the wall revealed wooden steps leading down. About two hundred feet below us, I saw a narrow sandy beach stretching to our left. The night before, when Lizzy took me to the port, I had seen only rocks leading down to the water.

"I didn't realize there were so many islands," I said. Some of them were fairly large, others only a big rock sticking out of the water. "Is that a house?" I pointed at a small island off to our right.

"Yeah. Most of the larger islands are owned by someone."

"I think it would be nice to live somewhere like that. It must be very quiet and peaceful."

Trevor laughed. "Save up your tips. That place sold for twenty million a couple of years ago. Included the whole island, though."

He took me to a restaurant a few blocks away that overlooked the bay.

"What do you like on your pizza?" he asked.

"What do they have?" I looked at the menu, trying to make sense of it. I had never had pizza, though I knew what it looked like. Food such as pizza and hamburgers wasn't served in the City, and although I had traveled extensively on missions for Master Benedict and the Hunters' Guild, my targets usually ate at fancy restaurants. I was comfortable with the food at Rosie's because I'd spent several months in Ireland on a mission.

"The usual stuff."

I glanced up at Trevor and realized he was looking at me strangely.

"Uh, whatever you like will be fine," I said.

A sudden grin appeared on his face. "Have you ever had pizza before?"

I felt my face warm. "Well…"

He laughed. "That's a first. Why don't you tell me what kind of food you don't like?"

With a shrug, my face suddenly feeling warm, I said, "I eat pretty much anything."

The waitress came, and he ordered a large pizza, half pepperoni and green peppers, half ham and pineapple.

"We'll give you a choice," he said.

It turned out that I liked both of them.

When we were through eating, I excused myself to the restroom, found our waitress, and paid our tab. I figured I could at least do that much for the help I was getting from Trevor, and I didn't want him to think we were on a date.

# CHAPTER 12

Instead of running along the creek behind my apartment the following morning, I took the train to the station by Trevor's house and jogged down to the beach. Running on sand was a pleasure compared with running on pavement.

High tide evidently swept the beach clean, because when I arrived at nine o'clock, mine were the first tracks on the sand. The beach curved out to a point of rock, and when I got to it, I found there was another sandy cove beyond, so I continued.

I had gone about half a mile when I smelled something that brought me to a stop. Scanning the area around me, I turned toward a silver-gray spot in the rocks above the beach. As I got closer, I could see the breeze causing a flutter in that silver spot.

Three wolves lay among the rocks with their throats torn out. Although I wasn't a wildlife expert, the wolves were very large, and I didn't think wolves hung out in urban areas. With those assumptions in hand, the logical conclusion was that they were werewolves. There was very little blood.

The cause of their deaths was uncertain, but it certainly appeared as though someone wanted them to look like vampire kills. Whoever killed them had received the same training I had in misdirection kills, but he was sloppy—or maybe arrogant would be a better description.

Other than their throats, the wolves didn't have a mark on them. There wasn't any indication of a fight. A mage might freeze the wolves or pin them down while he killed them, but a vampire wouldn't have that kind of power over a werewolf.

I turned and ran back to Trevor's house.

"Well, what a pleasant surprise," Trevor said when he opened the door.

"You have a thing for sweaty girls?" I asked. I had planned to go home and take a shower before coming back in the afternoon to check on his computer searches.

"If he doesn't, I do," I heard Josh's voice from inside the house. I rolled my eyes and gave Trevor what I hoped was a vexed expression.

"Can you call Lieutenant Blair for me?" I asked. "I think there's been a murder down on the beach."

"Murder?" Trevor echoed.

"Well, it might be better described as a massacre. You don't have any packs of real wolves here in the city, do you?"

He invited me in and made a call on his cell phone. After a few words, he handed the phone to me.

"Does he know where you live?" I whispered, holding my hand over the phone.

"He's a cop. He knows where everyone lives."

"Yes?" I said into the phone.

"What's this about a murder?" I heard Blair's voice.

"There are three very large, very dead wolves down by the beach near Trevor's house," I said. "I was running on the beach this morning and found them."

---

Josh and Trevor accompanied me back to where I'd found the wolves. When we got close, Josh asked, "How did you find them?"

My tracks were quite visible just above the water line, then they swerved away from the ocean toward the rocks.

"Smell. Can't you smell them?" I asked.

They both shook their heads. But when we got within about fifty feet, the breeze shifted directions, and Trevor said, "Oh, yeah. I smell them now."

"You've got a hell of a nose. Why were you down here?" Josh asked.

"I wanted to run on the beach. Be near the ocean. Around my place, there's just concrete and asphalt, and I might as well be in Kansas City. If I'm going to live near the ocean, then I ought to enjoy it occasionally, don't you think?"

"That's not the ocean. It's the bay," he said.

"Whatever."

"Is that where you're from?" Josh asked.

"Huh?"

"Kansas City."

"Oh, I was there once. They have a river but no ocean."

We waited for almost an hour for Blair and his people to show up. I spent the time looking for shells near the water. Trevor spent the time following me around, and Josh sat on the beach and watched us.

When the cops finally showed up, we met Blair at the entry point to the second beach. He gazed around at the area, then asked, "Did you disturb anything?"

I shook my head. "There weren't any tracks at all when I got here this morning, so we're responsible for all the ones you see."

"There was a high tide last night," Trevor said.

"You're sure they're werewolves and not coyotes?" Blair asked.

I shook my head. "You have a lot of coyotes the size of a St. Bernard or a Great Dane around here?"

Blair's cop shoes weren't the best thing for walking on loose sand, but he followed us, and a couple of detectives with his forensics team followed him.

"Yeah, those aren't coyotes," one of the detectives said. Blair drew his men aside, and I guessed he thought they were far enough away that I couldn't hear them.

"I recognize one of them," one detective said, "but they aren't from either of our packs. There's going to be hell to pay, though. Everyone's on edge with Carleton gone."

We watched the forensics team for about an hour, then the woman who seemed to be in charge came over to talk to Blair.

"Weirdest scene I've ever studied. No evidence of a fight, and other than the throat wounds, the wolves appear to be unharmed. There's also no blood. It's almost like they were killed somewhere else and teleported here. No tracks, either theirs or their killers', and it doesn't look like they were thrown from above. We'll have to do autopsies and tests, of course."

"Is teleportation even a thing?" Trevor asked.

Blair looked directly at me.

"I've never seen it," I said with a shrug, "but I never claimed to know everything." I winked at him. "It would really save on the transit passes though."

I noticed that he never answered Trevor's question. Thinking about it, levitation was something some mages could do. Aeromancers, like Frankie Jones.

The cops took our statements and let us go back to Trevor's house. I asked about the computer runs, and he said he needed time to winnow through all the results and he'd bring them by Rosie's that evening. I took the train back to my side of town and ran the last half mile to my apartment.

# CHAPTER 13

Werewolves were known for being hot headed, and the slaughter of three young wolves—rumored to be victims of a gang of rogue vampires—touched off a night of open battles across the city. Tending bar at Rosie's I heard a number of reports about it from customers coming in.

One of Blair's shifters who had been at the crime scene came in just before I got off work and asked for Sam.

"Sam isn't here," I said. "There's the shift manager and me." I went to the kitchen door and said, "Steve, cop out here."

Dworkin came out after a couple of minutes, wiping his hands on a towel. "What's up?" he asked.

"Checking in to see if you've had any trouble," the cop said. "And to warn you that it's not a safe night to be on the streets." He turned to survey the dining room, leaning back on the bar.

Steve looked at me.

"It's been quiet," I said. "There aren't very many

shifters who hang out at Rosie's, and I've only seen that one vampire in here."

"Yeah, but he died," the cop said, turning around to look at me. "Don't be surprised if the vampires remember that."

Dworkin gave me a ride home, not just to the apartment complex, but to the front door of my building.

"You all warded inside?" he asked as I got out of his pickup truck. "You know, anytime you think you need any help, all you have to do is ask."

"Yeah, I'm good." I gave him a smile. "Thanks, Steve."

I got a beer out of the fridge and stood out on my balcony, just enjoying the quiet of the night. It was cold, but I drew on the ley line for warmth. I stood out there for half an hour, and then I heard a wolf howl in the distance. It was answered by several more.

Shortly thereafter, I caught sight of three or four people walking down the path by the stream. They stopped when they came even with my building and looked up at me. Vampires. I smiled and silently toasted them with the beer bottle. After gathering in a circle and conversing a bit, they gave me another look and headed back in the direction they came from.

Supernaturals, as Sam called them, didn't worry me when I was home. Vampires and shifters had their own kind of magic, but they couldn't breach my wards. And since it was still light, I didn't have to worry about vampires when I went to work. But winter was approaching, and it would get dark earlier. Still, it was good to know that I was being watched so I could take precautions.

I finished off my beer and went inside to get ready for bed.

---

Blair and Frankie Jones were sitting at the bar talking to Sam when I showed up for work the following afternoon.

"You sure get around," Frankie said as I hung up my coat.

"Luck of the Irish," I responded. "How many dead shifters and vampires do you have on an average night?"

Neither she nor Blair answered. Blair squirmed a little.

"If you have to take off your shoes to count them," I said, "then maybe I'm unique only because I've reported the murders I stumbled across."

Sam gave me an appraising look, then smirked at Blair and Jones.

"What's the mood like at the Wolf's Den?" Sam asked. I knew that was one of the more popular shifter bars.

"Not good," Blair said. "There was a mini-riot at Full Moon around closing time, and The Shaggy Gentleman closed early. The owner of Necropolis isn't happy, either. She says business is way off because her regulars are sticking close to home."

I had heard of Necropolis, a vampire-goth nightclub that sounded a little too real for my tastes. "The Shaggy Gentleman?" I asked.

"Shifter strip bar," Sam said, motioning to the west. "About a mile that way on a dead end overlooking the river."

I don't know what my face looked like when he said that, but Frankie laughed. "Yeah, not a place I would hang out, either."

One of our regular customers came in, and Sam called out to him. It was the shifter-accountant that Jenny had pointed out to me when I first took the job. He came over and joined the conversation. Half an hour later, Josh and Jolene came in, and soon I counted fifteen people discussing the paranormal state of affairs in the city. All that talk was thirsty work, and they kept me busy.

It surprised me how openly everyone discussed things with Blair and Frankie there. Especially Blair. I guess he hung out at Rosie's often enough that people felt relatively comfortable with him.

"How do they keep the lid on this sort of thing?" I asked Lizzy when she came and sat at the other end of the bar, near the kitchen. The TV over the bar was tuned to the local news, and there wasn't a word about weird goings-on or bodies of wolves and decapitated vampires.

With a shrug, she said, "I don't think we've had something like this happen before." She studied the Tarot layout she had dealt. "Sometimes rival werewolf packs get into territorial disputes, but the vampires have always been pretty low-key. What scares me, though, is the Fae are getting restless."

I just stood there staring stupidly at her, not wanting what she said to be true. Most people—even witches and mages—tried to ignore the Fae, pretending they didn't exist. And for the most part, the Fae were fine with that. But I had run into the Fae more than once, and their magic was different and far more ancient than that of humans.

"Lizzy," I said, placing my hand on hers. She raised her face so I could see her eyes. "What do you See?"

She bit her lip. "Like I said, the Fae are getting restless. You know they only like disorder that *they* cause."

I nodded. "Yes, I know about the Fae. Control freaks, and they don't think the way humans do."

Lizzy nodded and went back to studying her cards. "You sure know a lot for a girl without any education."

I reached out and put my fingertips under her chin. "I didn't go to normal human schools, but I've read a lot, and I've traveled a lot. If you ever have questions about me, ask me. Asking someone else might get both of us killed. Just be sure only to ask questions you really want answered."

Our eyes locked, and I had no idea what she might be seeing when she looked at me, but after a minute, she gave me a trembling smile and said, "Will do."

I left her sitting there but came back a few minutes later and shoved a sloe gin fizz across the bar.

"Now, for a free drink, tell me about the Fae in this town."

Lizzy looked startled. She studied my face for a minute, then said, "There is a fairy mound northeast of the city just inside the national park. For the most part, a glamour and a warding spell keep everyone away, but there are lot of Fae living outside. I'd guess there are probably as many Fae living in the city as there are mages."

"Is the mound where the ley lines cross?" I asked.

"Just on the east side of the junction. There is a

small town of sorts above ground called Killarney Village, on the west side of the junction, and that is all Fae. So, the town and the mound are each bordered on three sides by a major ley line."

"And all this information about the Fae is common knowledge among the paranormals here?"

She blushed. "Not really."

"Just people who are related to them," I said. Her blush deepened. The night when we went out dancing and I found the Hunter, she gave directions to the taxi driver at the club to take her to 'Killarney Village'.

"It's probably not safe for you to go out there alone," she finally said.

"Got it. I'll be sure to arrange a tour guide if I decide to visit."

Lizzy blushed again.

Trevor came in later and handed me a folder filled with half an inch of paper.

"Here is what I found through my computer searches," he said. "I don't know if it's what you were looking for, or if it will do you any good."

I thanked him and bought him a drink. Later, when Steve Dworkin gave me a ride home, I took the folder with me and set it on the floor next to my bed, planning on reading through it the following morning.

---

Something was testing my wards. I came instantly awake, reaching for my sword. When my hand failed to find the sword, I realized where I was and leaped out of bed to the corner of the room, putting the wall behind me and pulling energy from the ley line running in front of the building.

In a near-panic, I crept toward the window, parting the blind a fractional amount so I could look out the window. The first light of dawn could be seen in the east. It took a few moments of scanning the scene below me to find a shadowy figure among the trees near the stream.

Another push against the wards, stronger than the first attempt. I fed a little energy into the wards to strengthen them but held most of the power I gathered in reserve. I searched for other presences but found only the one person. A third push came, then the figure below slipped away through the trees.

The clouds briefly broke, revealing the moon, and in that bare moment of light, I caught a good look at my attacker before the clouds closed again.

It was the Hunter. He had found me.

CHAPTER 14

Trevor had found quite a bit about the members of the Columbia Club and identified more members in addition to the ones I had found. Altogether, he gave me information on thirty people, all of them men, and in a note that he provided as a cover sheet for his research, he listed them and marked those he knew were paranormals or supernaturals. He found evidence that Lord Carleton had been a member, as was the alpha of a major Westport werewolf pack.

What he didn't find, or didn't document, was how the members communicated with each other, where they met, how often they met, or even if they ever met. Totally frustrating. If I was still a Hunter, with an unlimited credit card, I would simply pick one and follow him around until I knew what color toothbrush he used, let alone who he met with and screwed. But I had to eat, and work took up most of my week.

I went in to Rosie's and had lunch sitting at the bar. When the lunch rush wound down and Sam had some time, I told him what I suspected about the Columbia Club and what Trevor had found.

Sam was quiet while I talked, then said, "I'm not entirely sure where you're going with this."

"The Hunter showed up at my place last night and tested my wards."

"You're sure it was a Hunter?"

Shrugging, I said, "Three brute force attacks. Mage magic, not a spell. As to whether it was a Hunter, I'm pretty sure it was the same guy I saw who beheaded the vampire. Either him or someone dressed exactly like him, all in black, and carrying a sword."

"And how does that tie in to this Columbia Club?"

"Someone told him where I live. Now, who do Blair and Frankie Jones report to? Frankie's father and boss are members of that club." I pushed the member list Trevor compiled across the bar. "Maybe I'm paranoid, but I don't think these guys are getting together to play cards. I think someone is making a power move and called in a Hunter or some other kind of paranormal ninja to stir things up, and maybe take out any opposition. Sam, I don't know what all Blair and Frankie might know, but to my knowledge, I'm the only one who has actually seen the guy killing all these vamps."

Sam thought about it, then asked, "Did he physically try to get into your place?"

"No. You know that stream that runs behind the apartment complex?"

"Sloman's Creek."

"He was in the trees along the stream, a couple of hundred feet away from my apartment."

"And what would you have done if he breached your wards?"

"Run like hell."

He nodded. "Smart girl."

I would run if I could. For all I knew, he wasn't alone. Although some senior Hunters worked alone, most Hunters worked in pairs. A common tactic was to flush the quarry into an ambush by their partner. And Sam was right that I couldn't automatically assume the guy I saw in the alley downtown was the same one outside my apartment. If I faced a pack of them, I might as well jump in the ocean. I was good, but not that good, especially since I was unarmed. But the fact remained that someone told him where I lived. The vampires knew, the cops knew, and a few people at Rosie's knew. That sort of narrowed the list of possibilities.

Trevor came in that evening, sat at the bar, and ordered dinner.

"Did you tell anyone about the research I asked you to do?" I asked as I served him a beer.

"Nope. Why?"

"Not even Josh or Jolene?"

He shook his head. "Nobody's business but yours. I keep my customers by being discreet."

"The Hunter attacked my wards last night. Could anyone have detected the searches you did for me?"

"Absolutely not. My security is airtight, and I'm careful. Without going into detail, let's just say that if my methods could be detected, I'd be in jail by now."

I chuckled. "Either you're supremely arrogant, or you're really good, huh?"

He winked at me. "I'm good enough to be that arrogant. I'll tell you a little secret. Very, very few hackers are also electrokinetics. I have traps and protections laid that are undetectable by standard science. Anyone who tries to hack me or eavesdrop on me is risking a burned-out computer."

Which left me with my first guess—that Frankie had reported me seeing the Hunter, and what I had said about Hunters during her interrogations, to someone who cared.

---

Sam had an agreement with one of the nightclubs a block farther down the road that Rosie's employees could park in their lot. Steve Dworkin and I left work after our shift was over and walked to his truck, but before we got there, a dozen men stepped from the shadows. I shielded immediately. Getting accosted when I was tired at the end of my shift was getting very old.

"Are you the girl who found our packmates out on Southern Peninsula?" one asked. He had reddish-brown and white-streaked hair that fell over his collar, and a bushy beard to match.

"You know what I hate most about dealing with werewolves?" Steve asked me in a conversational tone. "Burning wolf hair really, really stinks."

A two-foot pyre of flame sprung from his open palm.

"Hey, wait! You got us all wrong!" the guy with red hair said. "We just want to ask the lady some questions."

"You obviously know where I work," I said. "You could have come in and asked your questions."

"Not our kind of place," another man with gray, frosty hair said.

"You need a dozen men to ask a little lady a question?" Steve asked.

"We travel in groups for protection," the first guy said.

"Didn't help your friends," I said.

The guy shook his head. "No, it didn't. Look, we didn't mean to scare you. Can we sit down and talk?"

I glanced at Steve, who said, "Come on back to Rosie's with us."

So, Steve and I and three of the shifters walked back to the bar. I noticed that the werewolves seemed to have more trouble walking through the door than Steve and I did.

We grabbed a table, and I took everyone's orders to the bar and brought the drinks back. The guy with frosty hair handed me two twenties and said, "Keep the change."

"The cops won't tell us shit," redhead said. "We were hoping you could tell us what happened."

"I was out jogging and found them in the rocks, about three feet apart, in a circle with all their heads facing inward. I don't know if that means anything to you, but it doesn't to me." I said. "Their throats were torn out, but the wounds were very clean. Almost no blood, and no other wounds that I could see. No signs of a struggle, no footprints. The police forensics lady said she didn't think it was vampires, and I agree with her. It looked staged."

They exchanged glances with each other, then frosty asked, "No signs of a struggle and no other wounds?"

I nodded. "That's right. For what it's worth, me not being an expert in dead wolves, I think whoever killed them immobilized them first, then slit their throats and worried the wounds to make it look like their throats were torn out. If the pathology reports don't show any drugs in their systems, then I would guess their killer used magic."

"And they were all completely shifted?" frosty asked.

I nodded. "I called the police because I didn't think wolves came into the city, and because of their size. I've seen a couple of real wolves, and they weren't anywhere near that big."

"And what kind of magic would it take to make a wolf hold still while you slit his throat?" the third guy asked.

I shrugged. "Put him to sleep or simply immobilize him. You know, just hold him in place." I turned to Steve. "I don't really know how to describe it in another way."

Steve shook his head. "I don't either." He turned to the shifters. "A witch would cast a spell, and a mage would draw power and wrap it around the person or creature he wanted to hold. It would be a terrifying way to die, unable to move while someone slit your throat. Much better if it was a witch casting a sleep spell."

"What kind of power would that take to hold three wolves while you killed them?" redhead asked.

I had been thinking about that since I found the bodies.

"I've no idea," I said. "I don't know if they were all killed at the same time, or even if they were killed where I found them. Any competent adult mage could probably manage to hold one wolf, but three? With no signs of a struggle or any wounds? Your guess is as good as mine."

I finally received a paycheck, so the following morning I took the bus to a bank Eleanor recommended, and then went to a grocery store. As I trudged home carrying four bags of food, Eleanor came out of the office with an envelope and tucked it into my coat pocket.

"A man was here earlier and left that for you," she said.

"What did he look like?"

"Fifties, dark hair, wearing a business suit. He was driving a fancy black car. I've never seen him before." She reached out and took two of my bags. "Let me give you a hand with that."

We carried the groceries up to my apartment, and I dissolved the ward on the door so Eleanor could come in. I put the food in the fridge and the cabinets, very aware of how empty everything was. Then I pulled out the envelope and looked at my name written in a flowing script.

I tore open the envelope and found a hand-written note in the same hand.

*Miss McLane,*

*I would be pleased if you could visit me tomorrow night at nine o'clock. 1743 Chelwood Lane.*

*Rodrick Barclay*

I turned the paper so Eleanor could read it. Her brow furrowed, and when her eyes rose to meet mine, there was a look of concern on her face. I waited.

"Rodrick Barclay is a vampire," she said. "He was

one of Lord Carleton's men. Came here with Carleton back in the 1880s."

"Great. I wonder what he wants. Unfortunately for him, I have to work."

Eleanor shook her head. "Talk to Sam. I'm not sure it would be good to ignore Barclay."

"You're not seriously suggesting that I go meet with him?"

"Not alone," she said.

So, when I got to work that evening, I handed Sam the note.

"Eleanor said a guy dropped this off for me this morning."

Sam read it and took a deep breath. "We can fiddle with the schedule. The question is, who do we send with you?"

"Seriously?"

He nodded. "I can drive you, but we need a fire mage to go with us. Someone who can put the fear of God into the bloodsuckers if necessary."

I thought about it. "Sam, I'm not afraid of vampires."

He opened his mouth as though he was going to say something, then stopped. Gradually he closed his mouth, then cocked his head to one side and gave me a raised-eyebrow look.

"I would be very grateful for a ride," I continued, "and I think if you came along, your reputation would make it much easier to walk out of there. I really don't want a fight."

He leaned back and stared at me for what seemed to be a long time, then said, "All you feel is a tingle when you come through the door?"

"Uh, yeah."

"I have that spell tied directly to a ley line."

I wasn't sure what he was getting at. "Yeah?"

"How much…" he stopped. "No, I don't want to know. Okay, I'll arrange the schedule. Come in at your regular time, and I'll have someone relieve you at seven."

## CHAPTER 15

The following evening, Sam and I climbed into his SUV and headed out to meet Rodrick Barclay.

"I looked Chelwood Lane up on a map," I said. "I assume Barclay thinks everyone owns a car." Barclay's home was on the northern edge of the city, in the foothills near the coast. Not only was it a long way from the nearest train station, it was a couple of miles from the nearest bus stop.

"Out in that part of town, everyone does own a car," Sam said.

We got on the east-west freeway, then took the northbound freeway at a major interchange. Within ten minutes, we left the parts of town I had seen before. After we crossed the river, the mountains, with their snow-capped peaks, grew closer. When we got near the foothills, Sam took an exit onto a parkway going west.

As soon as we crested the top of a hill, I could see the ocean before me, dotted with small islands, the river to the south, and beyond the peninsula where I'd found the dead wolves, more ocean. The city was very pretty at night, and I wondered what it looked like in the daytime.

Sam took a right, and we began to wind through narrower and narrower roads, then through the forest, climbing into the hills. Finally, he turned onto a road that didn't look wide enough for two cars to pass, and then we came to a stone wall with an arched gateway.

"This was Lord Carleton's estate," Sam said. "I wonder if all of his minions are still living here, or if Barclay won a power struggle."

Sam stopped the car, leaned out the window, and punched a button on a speaker box.

"State your business," the box said.

"Miss McLane to see Mister Barclay," Sam said.

The big iron-barred gate swung open, and we drove through. The road wound through more trees, and then the landscape opened up to reveal a large expanse of manicured lawn and what I assumed were flower beds, dormant now that winter was approaching. We drove around the garden to the Georgian manor house that stood as the centerpiece of the display. Obviously, Carleton had built a home such as he had in the days when he was alive—three stories of red brick with enormous windows that were twice as tall as a man. It was not the sort of house conducive to those with a severe sun allergy, but since he was never awake when the sun was shining, it probably didn't matter.

We parked in front, and the huge door opened. A man dressed as a butler stood there awaiting us.

"Cute little bungalow, don't you think?" Sam said with a chuckle.

"I've seen houses like this in Europe," I said, "but not too many of them in this country."

Having spent the past nine years living in what most people would consider a fantasy palace—inside what was essentially a medieval walled city—I was probably not as impressed as most American women my age would have been.

"Have you met any of the ancient vampires before?" Sam asked quietly as we climbed the front steps.

"Yes. I've met two who were much older than Carleton," I said. The master vampire I had killed in Austria was born in the twelfth century. His power was incredible, but he underestimated me, and I had been lucky. At the time, I was younger and very arrogant. After I got out of that scrape alive, my arrogance was greatly diminished. "Very scary. Not the sort of guy you'd want to anger."

"Even if Barclay is only a couple of hundred years old, you do understand the danger we're in. Right?" Sam said as we approached the door.

"Yeah. We're on the same page."

The butler was a vampire, of course, and looked to be in his sixties. I was aware that old vampires often rewarded their best servants by turning them, especially if the servant developed health issues.

The house was even more elegant inside than I would have expected looking at the outside. Hand-painted silk wallpaper, polished hardwood, parquet floors, cast plaster moldings, and very expensive artworks screamed money and eighteenth-century style. I felt rather shabby. I had put on my best white shirt and black trousers in anticipation of the meeting, but in that house, I felt I should be wearing a floor-length silk gown. Sam was dressed as he always did.

We passed a salon with at least twenty vampires and twice that many living humans having some sort of a party, and I saw more vampires watching us from the second- and third-floor mezzanines.

The butler led us into a large study with Persian rugs, ceiling-high bookshelves—particularly impressive when the ceilings were sixteen feet high—and a large desk. Two chairs sat in front of the desk with a low table between them. Two crystal glasses with a crystal decanter of what I assumed was water sat on a tray on the table.

"Miss McLane, Mr. O'Grady, how gracious of you to come," the man behind the desk said. He didn't rise to greet us. Dressed in a dark brown business suit with a red tie, he had piercing blue eyes and thick sandy hair that spilled over his collar. I judged that he'd been turned in his late thirties or early forties. Although it was difficult to tell with him seated, I guessed that he was in the six-foot range with an athletic body.

"Mr. Barclay," Sam said with a slight dip of his head. He took the seat on the left in front of the desk without waiting to be invited. Following his lead, I took the seat on the right.

"Would either of you care for water, or something stronger?" the butler asked.

"Water is fine for me," I said, and Sam nodded. I had no intention of eating or drinking anything served to me in that place. The butler poured liquid from the decanter into both glasses, then retreated to stand by the door.

"So, you're the young lady everyone is so excited

about," Barclay said. He looked me over, and I couldn't figure out from his expression if he was deciding whether to seduce me, merely drain me, or just kill me quickly and get it over with.

I fell back on my training. The Masters of the Illuminati had prepared me to rub elbows with royalty, heads of state, and captains of industry, all the better to get close to them and murder them. Barclay didn't intimidate me, and I was confident that if he did try to kill me, he would get the worse of the conflict. I was less confident that Sam and I would make it out of the place alive if that happened. There were dozens of vampires in the house, plus their human servants, and the guards at the gate were armed with submachine guns.

"I wasn't aware that I was such a person of interest," I said, giving him a sardonic smile.

"The rumor is that you're a Hunter," Barclay said, "or some other kind of legendary warrior."

"The rumor is that you're a vampire. Don't you find it amusing how such silly stories get passed around?"

The look Sam gave me was priceless, but Barclay threw back his head and laughed out loud.

"Oh, Miss McLane, I think I like you."

"Most people find me charming."

"So, you don't deny it?"

"I absolutely deny it. I'm a bartender." I leaned forward. "Mr. Barclay, I am a mage. I have a certain amount of training, and a certain amount of education. But I am not some sort of mythical creature seeking to save the world by going around slaying creatures of darkness. Now, why don't you tell me why you invited me here tonight?"

Barclay gave me the once-over a couple more times,

his sight lingering on my chest somewhat longer than was polite, then asked, "How much do you know about vampires?"

"More than I really ever wanted to."

"Very good. The Master of the City has suffered the final death. Someone—we think it was a Hunter—delivered that fate. There are now myself and three other mature vampires who were his children left to sort out his legacy. In addition, someone seems to be trying to pit the shifters and magic users against us. That could create a very uncomfortable situation for everyone should such conflicts become more public. Are you with me so far?"

"Yes, but I don't understand what that has to do with me."

"Ah. I have heard, and this is more than a rumor, that you have explained this exact scenario to Francis Jones and her team. I find it somewhat unsettling that a woman who appears so young and ordinary has such an in-depth understanding of such a complicated situation. Don't you find that unusual, Mr. O'Grady?"

Sam simply gave him a sour look and didn't respond.

"Miss McLane, do you understand what a nexus is?"

"The center of something."

"Yes. Why does everyone—the vampires, the shifters, the mages, the human civil authorities—all seem to be interested in you? Why do conflicts and murders occur wherever you happen to be? And why are you the only one—other than a couple of vampires centuries older than you are—who seems to understand what is happening? I believe you are a nexus. And if I'm correct, you're the only one who can keep everything from unraveling and exposing us to humanity."

Barclay rose from his chair and walked to a sideboard where he poured blood into a crystal goblet and took a sip. He was a bit shorter and perhaps more athletic than I had estimated. Probably a soldier, possibly a swordsman, when Carleton turned him.

He faced us and leaned back against the sideboard.

"Miss McLane, I will pay you a hundred thousand dollars if you can figure out what is going on and put a stop to it. Stop whoever is orchestrating this catastrophe that is about to descend on us all."

I took a deep breath and said, "I'm a bartender. I would love to have that much money, but I'm afraid you've mistaken me for something that I'm not. Now, if that is what you called me out here for, I'm sorry to disappoint you."

Barclay's face worked, seeming unable to decide whether he was sad, happy, or angry. "I'll make it a million!" he shouted.

I stood. "Sam, I think it's time for us to go."

"You can't do this! You have to help me! I'm the Master. Don't you want me to be the Master? Where are you going? Stop!" It was like watching a three-year-old throwing a tantrum. He stamped his feet and pounded his fists against the fireplace.

Sam stood and we walked out. The whole time we spent leaving the house, getting in Sam's SUV, and then driving out of the gate, I kept expecting something to go wrong, something to blow up, but nothing did. When we finally reached the public road and turned onto it, I heaved a sigh of relief.

"Good night! He's stark raving mad," I said. "I was afraid we weren't going to get out of there."

Sam glanced over at me and said, "You and me both. You've got a hell of a lot more balls than I gave you credit for."

We drove on for a while, then he said, "If you don't want to answer me, I'll understand, but I'm going crazy from curiosity. What is your affinity?"

I chuckled. "I don't have one." I thought about how much to trust him, but then decided that I had to trust someone, and he had been nothing but kind and supportive. "My father was a mage, and my mother was a witch. Somehow that all got intertwined. I'm a ley line mage without any affinity that I've ever been able to determine, and I can also cast spells, although I only know a handful. All my training is in manipulating ley lines."

He shot me a startled glance, then turned his eyes back on the road. "Give me an example of a spell you know."

"When I cast the wards on my apartment, I used a witch's spell, then reinforced it with energy from the ley line."

Sam barked out a laugh. "Now I know why you're so confident about your wards. That would confuse the hell out of me."

## CHAPTER 16

Too many people confused rationality with sanity. Master Benedict was the most rational person I'd ever met, but he was criminally insane. Obsessed with power, riches, and domination, there was nothing he wouldn't do to accomplish his goal of ruling the world.

And as rational as Barclay's analysis might be, that didn't change the fact that his goal was to become Master of the City, and old vampires were utterly ruthless. Getting in bed with him, either figuratively or literally, would be the craziest, stupidest thing I could possibly do.

What none of the people in Westport—remote from the world's power centers—understood was that their little tempest in a teapot was nothing compared to the goals and machinations of those Illuminati who were left alive. And I had no doubt that attracting the attention of the Illuminati would be disastrous.

Especially for me. I was willing to bet that I could count the number of Illuminati in Westport on one hand. If there were more than two, I would be shocked. But one thing I could never do was let them find me. If anyone who truly knew what the Illuminati stood for, who knew who I was, ever found out I was alive and what I had done, they would hunt me mercilessly. My only protection was ignorance of my survival. No one ever left the Order while still alive.

I was completely convinced that what I was seeing in Westport was due to one of the Illuminati. No one else could have called in a Hunter. I was also sure the Hunter had been assigned prior to the destruction of the City. To my knowledge—and my position under Master Benedict gave me insight most Hunters would never have—no Illuminati still alive in North America had the ability to contact, let alone assign, a Hunter. The Illuminati Council were the ultimate control freaks, and they were all in the City when it burned.

As a result, neither the Illuminati stationed in the city nor the Hunter had any way of communicating with their superiors because their superiors were all dead. Therefore, if I could take out the Hunter and the Illuminati stationed in Westport, the chaos would eventually sort itself out. No one was going to come looking for either one because no one knew they existed, but I had to do it soon in case my suppositions were wrong.

The meeting with Barclay told me that I was in a precarious position, with too much attention focused on me. I was attempting to keep my head down, but it seemed everyone thought I had something to do with the mess, and they weren't being quiet about it.

The night after our meeting with Barclay, three vampires walked into Rosie's. The first guy was the one who drew my attention. Tall and slender with thick black hair and blue eyes, he wore a tailored black suit that cost more than I made in a month. The other two were obviously his wingmen.

Mr. Tall-Dark-Handsome-and-Deadly headed straight to the bar and slid onto a seat while his buddies grabbed a table between the door and the bar, one sitting so he could watch the room, the other positioned to watch the door.

"What can I get you?" I asked. "We don't serve your usual drink."

"Macallan twenty-five," he said.

Probably our most expensive whisky. Sam had special glasses for such spirits, and when I set it on the bar, the vamp positively lit up. He lifted it to his nose and inhaled, then took a tiny sip and rolled it around on his tongue.

"I don't drink much anymore," he said with a musing tone in his voice, "but once upon a time I developed a taste for fine whisky, and sometimes I indulge myself." He pushed a hundred-dollar bill across the bar. I took it, rang up his drink, and gave him his change.

Most vampires didn't drink alcohol because their systems didn't process it very well, but I knew many of the older ones did. I had briefly worked in a club where the Bloody Marys were entirely too authentic.

He lifted his head, and I could tell he was scanning the bottles on our top shelf.

"The proprietor keeps a nice stock," he said.

"He has good taste."

His eyes dropped to my face and he said, "Yes, he does. Erin McLane?"

"You have the advantage of me, sir."

"George Flynn. I understand that you had a meeting last night with Rodrick Barclay."

"There aren't any secrets in this town, are there?"

Flynn chuckled. "Not too many. I don't suppose you would care to discuss your business with Rodrick."

"I don't have any business with Mr. Barclay," I said. "He simply wished to introduce himself."

"I see." He slid a business card across the bar. "Well, now I've also introduced myself. Changes are coming to Westport, and it never hurts to have friends. If you find yourself in need of a friend, I hope that you'll consider me. I think I could offer you far more than Rodrick can."

I shook my head. "I prefer to stay away from politics, especially supernatural politics."

"Sometimes events overtake us. I assure you, there are those in Westport who won't care about your preferences."

A customer came to the bar, and I went to take his order. After I mixed his drink, I turned back and saw that Trevor and Josh had taken seats on either side of Flynn, and the vampires sitting at the table weren't too pleased about it. I reached under the bar and wrapped my fingers around Sam's sawed-off baseball bat, feeling the jolt of magic that always came when I touched it.

Trevor was talking, but I couldn't hear what he was saying. Flynn seemed to be ignoring him, sipping his drink and looking straight ahead. After a few minutes, Flynn stood, laid a twenty on the bar, and walked away, his men following him out the door.

I walked over, picked up the twenty, and asked, "What was that about?"

Trevor shrugged. "Just reminding him that mages stick together, and that we would be very upset if anyone tried to harm one of us."

"I can take care of myself."

"I'm sure you can," Josh said, "but it never hurts to make sure the supes remember their place."

A couple of minutes later one of our regulars staggered through the door and announced, "There's a riot going on out there!"

"A riot?" Josh asked.

"Riot, battle, whatever you want to call it. Vampires fighting vampires. Must be thirty or forty of them."

Chairs scraped across the floor, and half of the people in the bar surged to their feet.

My training kicked in. Hunters were not only the soldiers of the Illuminati, but also the policemen, and while I had never done domestic duty, I had been trained to handle insurrections.

"Hold on!" I yelled. "Anyone who goes out that door isn't coming back inside!" Luckily, almost everyone paused. "I'm *not* having that mess come inside. Sam will *ban* anyone who brings a fight in here."

I grabbed Sam's magic bat and called, "Jenny! Cover the bar. Tell Steve what's going on and call Blair." Rounding the end of the bar, I told Trevor and Josh, "You two. Come with me."

They followed me out the door where we found a swirling battle of vampires fighting vampires. I saw Flynn near the entrance to our alley, and those vamps trying to get to him were discovering the difference between a young vampire and an old one. His hair was barely mussed as he grabbed a guy by the neck and twisted his head off.

"You guys stay here and cover the door. Don't do *anything* unless one of them tries to get to the door."

Casting a personal shield, I waded into the melee using the bat as I would a sword. Two men were fighting right in front of me. I hit the one with his back to me in the head, and when he fell, I clubbed the other one in the face. Another vampire, much taller than I was, came at me, and I broke his knees. The power embedded in the bat was pretty incredible, and I wasn't having to use any of my own power except to maintain my shield.

While the vamps seemed to know who their enemies were, I didn't care. I took out three more before they seemed to notice me and consider me a threat. Several turned to face me.

The fight was rather quiet, and when I raised my voice, it carried. "Stop this! Now! Get the hell out of here!"

Most of them stopped what they were doing and gaped at me.

"If you want to act like a bunch of juvenile delinquents, do it somewhere else. The police are on the way."

One guy leaped at me, a sneer on his face. I poured power into my hands, and the bat changed his expression. Everyone watched him fly across the street and slam into the hotel wall.

"I'm not joking. Get the hell out of here before I start killing people."

"Don't piss the lady off," Flynn said. "Come on. Let's go."

About a third of the vampires retreated toward

Flynn, and then their group began to back out of the alley onto the main street. The others seemed torn between watching Flynn and watching me.

The sound of sirens in the distance, coming closer, seemed to get everyone moving, and in less than a minute, the street was empty of all but five vampires, and they weren't in any shape to move. One was missing a head and two were missing their hearts. I had seen an old vamp do that before—plunge his hand into someone's chest and pull his heart out. The guy whose knees I'd broken and the guy I'd hit a home run with weren't in any shape to move, either.

I turned toward the door and walked between Josh and Trevor. "Come on. Let's get inside. I don't want to be out here when the cops show up."

One of the things Rosie's didn't have was windows, so there weren't any witnesses other than the two mouseketeers. When we got back inside, I said, "I would appreciate it if you didn't mention what happened out there."

"Jesus, Erin, you're a major badass," Josh said.

"Here, touch this," I said, pushing the bat at him. He reached out and grabbed it, then jerked his hand back, his eyes wide. I grinned. "Sam gave me this when I asked about bouncers. Pretty impressive, huh?"

Of course, everyone in the bar was watching us. Raising my voice, I called, "All over. Just a bunch of stupid vamps dancing with each other, and they don't dance worth shit."

That brought a laugh, and when I walked behind the bar and put the bat away, I called, "Half-price drinks for the next fifteen minutes to celebrate our victory in the Battle of Rosie's Alley!"

Josh went outside when we heard the sirens, and then came back in to report that five cop cars had shown up, and one TV news car.

After the fifteen minutes were over and everyone had a drink, I said to Jenny, "Can you cover for me a minute?"

I walked back into the kitchen, sat down in a chair, and let the adrenaline and power flow out of me.

"Hey, are you okay?" Steve asked. He was standing over me, and I realized I was shaking.

"Yeah. Just reaction."

He walked out to the bar area, and when he came back, he was holding a glass of whiskey.

"Here, drink this."

I did, and by the time the burn of the liquor hit my stomach, the shakes stopped.

"Thanks," I told him.

After a couple of minutes, I went back to my place behind the bar and waited for Lieutenant Blair. He didn't disappoint me, showing up ten minutes later.

"What the hell happened?" Blair asked before he even reached the bar.

"Good evening to you, too, Lieutenant? Coffee?"

He shook his head.

"Josh said the press showed up. Did you give them an interview?"

Blair rolled his eyes. "Frankie is taking care of them. We're reporting it as a gang fight."

"I'm sure businesses around here will appreciate that. Nothing like roaming gangs in an area to attract customers."

If looks could kill, I was fairly sure I at least would

have been crippled. I took pity on him before he dragged me down to his office again.

"Ms. Jones is correct," I said. "Two gangs of vampires decided to have a brawl outside. I assume they didn't like each other for some reason, but no one came in to tell me why they did it, or why they picked here."

"Were any of them inside before it started?" he asked.

"Yes, a gentleman with a very pale complexion came in for a drink. He likes our selection of whiskies. As far as I know, the fight started after he left."

"So, no one in here was involved?"

I shook my head. "I threatened to tell Sam to ban anyone who went outside."

Blair chuckled. "You're a hard woman, Ms. McLane."

I gave him a grin. "I can be. Would you want to try and explain to Sam why his bar got busted up?"

"Not a chance."

I considered telling him about all the attention I was getting from shifters, vampires, and the Hunter but decided to keep my mouth shut. I didn't think Blair was the one putting me in danger, but he reported to Frankie. And some of what Barclay had said came from a conversation I had with Frankie when Blair wasn't present.

Blair spoke to Trevor and Josh on his way out, and I saw both of them shake their heads. Blair didn't look pleased. Once he left, I poured a couple of drinks and walked down the bar.

"On me," I said as I pushed them across the bar to Trevor and Josh. "Thanks for having my back."

"No problem," Trevor said.

"Damn," Josh said, "did you see that one guy twist that vamp's head off? Like opening a jar."

I nodded. "Older vampires have an incredible amount of power, and it just increases with age."

"How long do they live?" Josh asked.

"Until someone kills them, or they commit suicide," I answered. "I've been told some of them are thousands of years old."

## CHAPTER 17

I was left with the problem of what to do about all the attention I was receiving. With Flynn's appearance, that problem was obviously getting worse. I could always leave town, but I didn't have enough money to go very far, and I'd have the problem of how to eat and find a place to live in a new town with even less money than I had when I arrived in Westport.

As a Hunter, I was trained in determining who needed to be removed to resolve a particular situation. That often required weeks or even months of stalking suspects, following leads through social and business networks, and working my way into position to quietly take care of the problem individuals. Mass slaughter was rarely a good idea and bound to attract attention. Identifying the one or two people who were causing the problems in Westport and taking them down was a far better solution.

But I didn't have the time or the money to take a Hunter's patient approach.

Steve drove me home after work, but when he pulled

up in front of my building, I saw a red sports car parked in the space assigned to me if I had a car. Frankie Jones had driven a car like that the day I found the dead werewolves.

Sure enough, when I got out of Steve's truck, Frankie got out of the sports car and approached me.

"May I have a word, Ms. McLane?"

"It's late," I said. Not to mention it was cold and drizzling.

"I know," she said. "But I would appreciate a little of your time."

I thought about it, then said, "Let's go inside."

I dissolved the ward on my apartment door and let her in, then re-cast the ward. If it was a setup, she would have to deal with me one-on-one. I wasn't going to provide a hole in my defenses if she had people with her.

She looked around at the lack of any furniture. I had my eye on a small dinette set at Goodwill but was waiting until after I paid the rent and got my next paycheck.

"I love what you've done with the place," she said. "Sort of a minimalist feng shui?"

"Yes, it's the chic look that's very in with the broke-bartender set."

I took off my coat and hung it in the closet by the door. I didn't offer to hang hers.

"About tonight," Frankie said. "I understand that George Flynn came into Rosie's to see you tonight."

Obviously, she had at least one informant in the bar. I didn't think it was Josh or Trevor, so I would have to figure out who else might be tattling on me.

"He came in for a drink," I said.

159

"I suspect that brawl was between Flynn's adherents and those of Rodrick Blaine, who I understand you also know."

I went into the kitchen and put the teakettle on the stove. "You seem to know everything about me," I said.

"Are you aware that a TV news team showed up tonight?"

"So I heard."

"They were tipped off," she said. "I thought at first they might have been monitoring the police frequencies with a scanner, but one of them admitted they received a phone call telling them something was going to happen at the Huntsman Hotel. Ms. McLane, I don't think I need to tell you how bad it would be if the paranormal world was revealed."

I shook my head. "No, you don't. Tea?"

She hesitated a moment, then said, "Yes, please."

"Ms. Jones," I said as I pulled a pair of mugs from the cabinet and dropped tea bags in them, "I don't know what you want from me. I'm just a bartender, and I barely know any of the players in this city. And I'll tell you honestly that I have no intention of getting involved. I just wish all of you would leave me alone."

"I'm sure you think that," she said, "but you're involved whether you like it or not."

That pissed me off. I turned to her, "And that's your fault. Every damned thing I tell you is being passed along to people who are hassling me. Your damned questions are getting repeated to me by vampires I've never met before. Shape shifters, and who knows who else, are stopping me on the street, and coming around here trying to break in. Are you trying to get me killed? Every time I talk to you, I can count on someone showing up who I don't want to know."

The teakettle started whistling, and I poured water into the mugs.

Handing her one of the mugs, I said, "Whoever you're talking to is stirring the pot, hoping to take some kind of advantage of the chaos that's infesting this city. Rodrick Barclay repeated to me, practically verbatim, a conversation you and I had. He wanted me to find the Hunter for him."

She rocked back on her heels, a shocked expression on her face. "What did you tell him?"

I wondered if she was as crazy as Barclay. "What do you think? Do I look suicidal? How in the hell would I find a Hunter if the entire damned police force can't? Go out and walk down dark alleys at night hoping he shows up? And then what would I do?"

I pulled the tea bag out of my mug and tossed it in the trash.

"I wish I had picked another city," I said. "If I knew this place was so crazy, I would have."

"So, why did you come here?"

Because of the ley lines. Because I would be far more powerful in Westport than most other places if the Illuminati found me. Because it was some place I'd never been before, and for that reason, no one had any cause to look for me there. Of course, that wasn't something I was going to tell her.

"This is as far as I could afford a bus ticket," I said.

She opened her mouth to say something, but then just shook her head. She looked around my empty apartment, and I hoped she would see the logic of what I told her. The truth was, I had almost run out of money. I could always rob a bank, or an armored car, and probably get away with it. I had done so many things that were much worse. But I hoped to make a clean break with my past. If it wasn't for the Hunter, I wouldn't even care about all the crap going on around me.

Frankie set her mug on the counter. "I'm sorry I bothered you."

I had to dissolve the ward again to let her out. I noticed that she never did address the issue of Barclay and others coming after me. Shaking my head, I went back into the kitchen, picked up my mug, and took a sip of my tea.

An explosion rocked the building. The dishes in my cabinets rattled, and I almost lost my balance. *What in the hell now?*

No, I decided, not in the building, but outside. I rushed out of my door and ran down the hall, looking out the window at the parking lot below. Frankie stood near the burning wreck of her car, surrounded by three men. One of them hurled a fireball at her, and it splashed off her shield.

My first thought was that she was going to pay a price for being mistaken as me. Then logic kicked in, and I realized only a blind man would mistake Frankie Jones for me. But they were attacking her in my parking lot, which didn't make a lot of sense.

I rushed down the stairs and out the front door. A small whirlwind blew across the parking lot, engulfing one of the men facing Frankie and knocking him off his feet.

With one exception, my magic was good only for a limited distance. While someone like Josh might be able to throw a fireball a hundred yards, my range was about fifty feet. Running forward, I hit the nearest mage with a burst of energy that tossed him to the ground like a rag doll.

The guy who hurled the fireball turned toward me and let another one go. I dodged it and pushed another burst at him. It knocked him head over heels.

Then the man who was knocked down by the mini-tornado hurled an orange ball of energy at Frankie. It hit her shield and rocked her back. He was too far from me for my magic to reach him, and I had other problems as both of the guys I had knocked down scrambled to their feet.

I rushed the nearest mage, and our shields met. I was sure he expected me to bounce off him, but he was disappointed. I punched through his shield and crushed his chest. His shield dissolved.

Picking him up, I threw him at the second man, who was just unleashing a fireball in my direction. It hit his buddy, engulfing him in flames.

Before the pyromancer could call another fireball, I stepped toward him and kicked him in the balls, lifting him four feet off the ground. He fell in a heap and lay still.

The mage facing Frankie turned toward me and let loose with another one of those orange balls. I dodged and it grazed my shield. I felt it, which surprised me, so I pulled more power from the ley line.

Before I could move on him, a powerful gust of wind hit him, sending him staggering backward. When he gained his balance again, he looked back and forth at Frankie and me, then turned and ran. Another gust of wind knocked him off balance, but he managed to keep his feet.

I didn't feel like chasing him. I looked at Frankie, who seemed to be okay, and turned my attention to the men on the ground. The one who caught the fireball was certainly dead, the magefire still burning as his body blackened. The other guy wasn't offering to get up. I thought I had felt bones break when I kicked him, so it was likely he couldn't walk.

"Are you okay?" I called to Frankie.

"Yes," Frankie said, walking over to where I stood over my victim. "Is he alive?"

About that time, the guy threw up, signaling that indeed he did survive.

"Yeah, but I think he might need a doctor. What happened?"

"I unlocked my car, and a fireball hit it. If I hadn't shielded in time, I think the explosion might have killed me. Knocked me down. Then these three came out of the shadows and attacked me."

"Does your insurance cover paranormal attacks?" I asked.

She gave me a startled look, then laughed. "That's a very good question."

I cast a ward around the survivor to hold him in place, just in case he wasn't hurt so badly that he could crawl off, and we went back inside. We stood in the hallway, and Frankie made a phone call.

Eleanor showed up a minute later, and a number of people who lived in the complex came out to gawk. A couple of my neighbors who lived in my building came out of their apartments and asked Frankie and me if we were all right. Everyone had questions that we didn't answer.

Some of the cops from Blair's team showed up, along with a truck from the fire department, and it was near dawn before I finally got to bed. The one positive thing was that Frankie deflected the cops and I didn't have to give a statement.

"The last thing I want is for anyone to hear about what happened," she said.

CHAPTER 18

Frankie came in to Rosie's the following evening around nine o'clock and sat down at the bar.

"What's your pleasure?" I asked.

"A vodka and tonic and a menu," she replied. She looked completely worn out. I didn't think she'd had much sleep.

I made her drink and handed her a menu. "Are you driving?"

She started, looked down at the drink in her hand, and said, "Yeah. I am. I've got a city car."

I stuck out my hand.

After a moment, she reached in her purse and handed me a pair of keys on a ring with a paper tag. I glanced at the tag and saw a printed line, "City of Westport," along with what looked like a license tag number.

"I'll call you a cab when you're ready to leave," I said. "I recommend the salmon special. I liked it so much the first time I had it, I applied for a job."

The look she gave me was so weary I wanted to give her a hug, but instead I just gave her a grin.

"How can I beat a recommendation like that?" she asked, making an effort to smile back at me.

I watched her gulp half of her drink and poured her a glass of water. I put the water on the bar along with a small glass vial with a hand-written label. Energy Enhancer.

"As long as you don't tell the Liquor Control Board or the FDA," I said. "The cook's wife is a witch and an apothecary. A very adept one, I must say."

Frankie unscrewed the cap and downed the potion. "Thanks," she said. "And thank you for last night."

I shrugged. "Hard to sleep with all that noise going on. If you don't put your foot down, people will think they can go around blowing up cars without any consequences."

She took another pull on her drink. "The guy we arrested has a long rehab ahead of him. Pelvis broken in four places and a dislocated hip. The doctors removed his testicles. They were completely crushed. Remind me never to piss you off."

I winked at her. "Too late, you already have."

Frankie nodded. "I did hear you last night. I'm still trying to process what you told me."

I left her to take a drink order, and by the time I checked on her again, Donny was placing her meal in front of her. She raised her empty glass to catch my eye, and I mixed her another drink.

"This really is extraordinary," she said, gesturing with a fork full of salmon when I took her drink to her.

"Yeah. The food here is really good. Steve is a wizard in the kitchen."

"I'll have to come in more often," she said. "You know, the one thing that puzzles me is why those idiots didn't shield themselves. The coroner said the guy who burned was dead before the fireball hit him. Crushed chest, and his heart exploded. And then the other guy." She shook her head and took another bite.

I didn't see any reason to tell her that they were shielded. But they drew on the ley line for their power, and that was my playground. It was equally easy for me to draw ley line energy from another mage as it was to draw it from the ley line directly. Their shields didn't shield against me but fed into my power. A witch's shielding, which didn't draw on the ley lines, was another matter.

That didn't mean I could absorb the energy of a fireball or those exploding orange balls the guy who got away was conjuring. Once a mage created a weapon like that, it was no longer connected to the ley line, and I would burn as readily as anyone else.

"I take it you haven't questioned him yet," I said.

Shaking her head, she finished chewing and said, "He was in surgery most of the day. The doctors say we might be able to talk with him in two or three days."

Frankie hung around for a couple of hours, then I called her a cab. In spite of the potion, I didn't think she should be driving, and she didn't ask for her keys back.

After she left, Lizzy came up to the bar and sat down.

"You might think about using arcane means to find the man you're looking for," she said.

I did think about it as I mixed drinks and pulled beers, occasionally glancing at Lizzy as she sat there reading something on her phone.

Finally, I planted myself in front of her and said, "How do you think I could do that?"

A sly smile grew on her face. "You do know some people who find things."

"Things. And people?"

Lizzy nodded.

"Would those people who can find things include you?"

She winked. "Sometimes. Who exactly are you looking for?"

I pulled out of my pocket the list Trevor had compiled and unfolded it. "I'm thinking that someone on this list summoned the Hunter. I'm also interested in who has been blabbing all over town that I'm connected to him. I'm not sure it's the same person."

"Let me think about it. Can you leave the list with me for a while?"

"Yeah, think I've got it memorized."

"Okay. You probably want to talk with Jolene as well."

Trevor and Josh came in later, but Jolene wasn't with them. I pulled Trevor off to the side and asked him, "Do you think, with the information you gathered for me, it would be possible to find out which of the men in the Columbia Club is orchestrating this whole uproar in the supernatural communities?"

He scratched his chin and looked thoughtful. For some reason, he looked more handsome in that moment than he did when he was trying to flirt and impress me.

"I don't know," he said. "It's an interesting question."

"Lizzy suggested that I talk to Jolene."

Trevor turned and looked down the bar to where

Lizzy still sat playing with her Tarot cards. "I'll tell Jolene to come see you."

"I thought you guys were all joined at the hip, but I haven't seen her in a while."

"New boyfriend, and he's a norm." He turned back to me. "You know, Jolene and Lizzy together might be able to pull something like that off."

———

Jolene came into the bar alone the following afternoon, right after I started my shift.

"Trevor said you wanted to talk with me."

Suddenly embarrassed, I said, "Well, I was hoping I might be able to use your professional services, but I don't have any money."

"Well, why don't you tell me what you want, and we'll figure something out. Free drinks for a year or something."

"It's a little complicated to explain right now. Maybe I could come by tomorrow, or you could swing by my place, and I can show you what I've got."

She nodded and slid a ten across the bar to pay for her drink. "That will work. Got a pen?" She wrote an address on a piece of paper and gave it to me. "Stop by around eleven."

"On me," I said, shoving the ten back to her. She smiled and held up her glass to toast me.

That night, I wrote out the list of members of the Columbia Club and added it to the folder of information Trevor had given me. With that done, I got ready for bed, but before I climbed beneath the covers, I felt a push against my wards—much stronger than the night the Hunter visited me. I tumbled out of bed and crawled across the floor, casting my personal shield for protection in case the wards fell.

I peered through the blinds of the sliding-glass door to my balcony and almost had a heart attack. The Hunter was there, standing on the balcony, less than five feet away from me, with his unsheathed sword in his hand. A sword that I knew could probably pierce my shield.

A second push, even stronger. Not sure what to do, I pulled power from the ley line and backed away from the door, prepared to do battle. I wasn't dressed, but that wouldn't stop me from bolting out the front door if he made it inside. Nothing happened. I waited a few minutes, then cautiously made my way back to the balcony door and peeked through the blinds again. The Hunter was gone.

I sat up for another hour, coiled like a spring waiting for something to happen, but nothing did. Finally, I turned out the light and went to bed, but it was a long time before I managed to fall asleep.

After checking my trusty map, I took the bus to the train station, then took the train to Jolene's place. That put me six blocks closer than taking the bus.

She lived in a small cottage about a mile from downtown and a mile from the port. A compact car sat in the driveway in front of the garage.

The neighborhood looked to be 1950s, all the houses about the same size on large lots. A couple of places, however, were new—two-story McMansions that almost covered the lots they were on. One of the houses on the corner of the next street over from hers was being demolished, I assumed to build another of the huge homes that stood out so much from their neighbors.

"I love your house," I said when she invited me inside. It really wasn't any larger than my apartment, but the yard showed a lot of flowerbeds and what looked to be a vegetable garden in the back, visible through the kitchen window. I wondered if I might ever have such a lovely, cozy place to live.

"Yeah, so do I. Unfortunately, I'm just renting, so I dread the day my landlady dies. She's in her eighties, and I'm sure her daughter will sell the place to one of the property monsters as soon as she can."

I showed her the research Trevor had given me and explained my suspicions about the Columbia Club.

"So, you want to know who the black widow sitting in the middle of the web is," Jolene said.

"Exactly."

"Interesting problem. Any guesses?"

"Frankie's boss—the District Attorney—and the mayor's chief of staff are my first guesses. I'm assuming she reported what is going on up the ladder. The attack on her at my place kind of reinforces that."

"Makes sense," Jolene said.

"Do you mind my asking? I've heard of finders, and I always thought they were witches."

Jolene laughed. "It's sort of complicated. Our dad is a mage, a pyromancer like Josh, and our mother is a witch." She brushed at her hair with her hand. "We get the red hair from her. But things got all intertwined with me. I'm a witch, but I can draw on the ley lines to enhance my spells."

"No kidding? I'm a ley line mage, but I can cast a few spells, and then I enhance them." I had never run into anyone else like me. The Illuminati said that my mix of talents was extremely rare.

She took me into the garage through a door off the kitchen and showed me her laboratory. A circle enclosing a pentagram was painted on the concrete floor. Stands holding black candles surrounded the circle. Counters and a pair of sinks lined the walls next to an old gas stove and the clothes washer and drier. Cabinets lined the other wall. The garage door looked as though it wouldn't open and was insulated with fiberglass insulation and Styrofoam.

I shook my head. "I've never had any real training in witchcraft. I wouldn't know what to do with any of this stuff."

Jolene dipped her head, her hair sliding forward to hide her face, and she hunched her shoulders. Her voice fell in volume, almost as though to dismiss what she said next. "If you want to learn, I'd be glad to teach you. I'm not an apothecary or an alchemist, but I'm good at a lot of useful stuff."

"I would love that," I said. "I love learning anything."

Her head came up, and she seemed to search my face, as though to see if I was serious.

"Sure," she said. "If you like, we could set up some time and I can show you a few things."

"And hope I don't blow up your house."

She laughed.

"Trevor said something about you and Lizzy together might be able to figure out who the black widow, as you call him, is."

Jolene turned her gaze up to the ceiling and was quiet for a very long time. "You know, sometimes that boy has some good ideas. You do know about Lizzie, don't you?"

I wasn't sure what she was getting at. "I know she's a seer, and a clairvoyant, and a genius."

"And her hair isn't dyed."

"Oh. I hadn't thought about it, but I knew that she lives out in Killarney Village, and I was told that is a Fae town."

"Yes, it is. Her father was a witch, and her mother, well, isn't human. Look, let me read through all this stuff you brought me and try a few things, and if I think Lizzy could be helpful, I'll let you know."

We agreed to meet for lunch the following week and give me my first witchcraft lesson, and she said she would come by the bar and let me know if her investigation turned up any information about my mystery man.

## CHAPTER 19

Jolene, Trevor, and Lizzy came in during the dinner rush, looked around for a table, then decided to sit at the end of the bar closest to the door.

"We're here to work on your project," Jolene announced when I approached them.

"Where's Josh?" I asked.

"He has a date," Trevor said.

I raised an eyebrow, and Jolene laughed. "They're going to a hockey game. He seems to have found a woman who shares his interests."

They ordered dinner and drinks, then Jolene pulled out Trevor's folder and the three of them bent their heads over it. I checked on them occasionally, and once or twice they asked me questions, but otherwise they didn't seem to need my input.

After I cleared away their dishes, Jolene said, "Lizzy thinks the mayor's chief of staff is the villain. But you don't really need to find him. We know where he lives and works. What we need to find is the Hunter. Right?"

"Why the chief of staff?" I asked.

"I See him," Lizzy said. She shrugged. "When I went down your list and looked up their pictures on the internet, he gives me a buzz. And when I visualize the Hunter with all of their pictures, he's the one who feels right."

It might not be scientific, but magic wasn't science. I remembered someone asking me how I knew where to find a ley line. There wasn't a way in the world I could explain it. I just felt them.

Trevor said, "I mean, the Hunter is just a person. He has to eat and sleep someplace. Right?"

"Yeah," I said. "He's a mage, but still human."

"So," Jolene said, "if we can find him, we can take him down."

"Uh, we? You mean the whole damned bar?"

They all laughed. "We'll let Blair and Frankie figure that part out," Trevor said.

Sure, I thought, and let the Hunter slaughter their whole little paranormal crime group. To be honest, I wasn't sure what I could do if I did confront the Hunter. I was a little bit puzzled that he was so cautious about me. I had never worried that one of my targets might best me. Even William Strickland had little chance against me, and he was one of the most powerful mages I'd ever encountered.

"Do you know anyone who's good at trap spells?" I asked.

Jolene looked thoughtful, then said with a laugh, "I do pretty good trapping mice, but I've never tried to trap a mage. Sam might know someone."

I glanced at Lizzy, but she shook her head. "You don't want the kind of help I could find."

The Fae never did anything for free, and the payment they would ask had nothing to do with money.

"Right," I said. "I'll talk to Sam. You'd think Blair would have someone like that on his team."

Trevor shook his head. "Most paranormals don't want to get involved with Blair. I've gotten the impression that his budget could handle more people, but he has a hard time recruiting."

Since I was one of the people he'd tried to recruit, I understood. As Westport had demonstrated, sudden death in the magical world was all too common. Only a fool stepped in between warring paranormals or supernaturals unless they had no other choice.

Lizzy and Jolene stayed for a couple of hours more, then they took off. Trevor stuck around, flirting and talking to me when I wasn't busy. He walked me out to the bus stop when I got off work, saying he'd ride the bus to the train station.

"The offer to buy you dinner is still open," he said as we walked.

He was handsome and seemed very nice. I did know that I felt comfortable with him, but I wasn't sure I was looking for a romantic relationship. Hell, I didn't know what a romantic relationship entailed, other than what I'd seen in a few movies.

"Trevor, I like you a lot, but my life is so crazy right now. I don't want to lead you on. Hell, I don't know what I'm doing or what I want."

He gave me a smile. "Have you had west coast crabs?"

"No." I actually couldn't remember ever eating a crab. They weren't on the menu in the City of the Illuminati, situated in a forest near the Canadian border. Trout, muskellunge, and walleye were the fish I knew.

"Let me take you out as a friend. Show you a little of Westport." He cocked his head, a slight smile on his face. "No expectations. Okay?"

"Oh, hell," I said with a smile. "Okay. I'm off on Mondays through Wednesdays."

"Next Tuesday, then," he said. "I'll pick you up at your place."

We got to the bus stop about five minutes early. I dropped onto the bench and looked around in time to see the Hunter emerge from the trees behind the stop. Dressed in a black, skin-tight bodysuit with a balaclava covering his head, he would have been almost invisible except for his movement and a flash of light reflecting from his sword.

"Shield!" I called out, casting my own shield as I leaped to my feet.

Lightning shot from Trevor's hands and created a fireworks show as it hit the Hunter's shield.

The Hunter ignored him, heading directly toward me with his sword unsheathed. I pointed at him and said a Word, casting the same spell I'd used to kill the vampire my first night in Westport. My magic wasn't showy, and no one could see it, but I knew when his shield deflected it. It rocked him for a moment, but then he kept on coming.

The Hunter was armed, I knew, with a spelled short sword or long knife in addition to his spelled sword, and had a half-dozen knives and a dart gun. I had no weapons at all. When he got closer, I dodged, diving to my left and forward under his sword. My quickness took him by surprise, and he continued for a couple of steps before he stopped and whirled.

I crashed into his legs, knocking him down. It took him by surprise, as he expected his shield to protect him, but my shield absorbed his shield's energy. Before he could recover, I kicked him in the head, then leapt away.

Another bolt of lightning, condensed and focused, hit the man on the ground. He rolled away, but the following bolt also found him. He fought to get up, but I could tell he was weakened, staggering a little as he found his feet.

Deciding that Trevor was a threat, he hurled a fireball in my friend's direction. Trevor ducked it and let loose another lightning bolt, forked into four prongs. Two of them hit the Hunter.

He turned his head in my direction, and I could tell he was calculating a charge at me, but I was fifteen feet away.

The lights of the bus approaching illuminated the scene. The Hunter turned his head and saw the bus coming toward us, then gathered himself, tossed something at me, and sprinted away in the direction of the trees.

I backed up as fast as I could and saw the ball the Hunter had thrown hit the ground. Smoke or gas exploded from the ball, and I tweaked my shield, making it airtight.

The bus slowed to a stop past the smoke, and Trevor and I ran to catch it. We boarded and showed our transit passes; the driver closed the door and pulled back onto the street.

I dropped into a seat, and Trevor plopped down beside me.

"So, this is how you get your exercise?" he asked. "Definitely saves on paying for a gym membership."

I laughed, and it sounded shaky even to me. "Not my preferred workout."

"So, that's a Hunter?"

"Yeah."

"Nasty. If anyone ever accuses you of being paranoid, tell them to talk to me."

We rode for a little while, then I said, "You're a badass. Who would have thought?"

He chuckled. "I can stick up for myself. Had to face an ogre once. He lost."

"I'll bet you're a major hit at Fourth of July parties."

I felt his hand on my face and turned to look at him. He leaned forward and kissed me. A very gentle, very full kiss. Lots of lip and only a bare touch of tongue. Then he pulled back and smiled.

I was stunned. And speechless. No one had ever kissed me like that before.

"Wh-what was that for?" I finally managed to say.

"Your knight in shining armor claiming his prize for rescuing the damsel in distress."

In the back of my mind, something was saying, *That's awful damned cheeky. Who says I was in distress?* But I didn't really feel that way. I thought it was sweet, and I wanted him to do it again.

The bus pulled up to my stop. Trevor stood to let me out.

"Should I walk you in?" he asked.

"No, I don't think he can run as fast as the bus. I'll be okay."

We stared at each other, and then I said, "I-I don't think going out on Tuesday is a very good idea."

I spun about and rushed to get off the bus. Halfway across the parking lot, I turned and watched the bus pull away. I could still feel his lips on mine, and my head was spinning more from the kiss than it was from the Hunter's attack.

CHAPTER 20

A pounding interrupted my sleep. At first, I couldn't figure out what it was, but when it stopped, I drifted back to sleep. Then it started again. Groggily sitting up, I figured out it was someone knocking on my door. No one had ever knocked on my door.

Throwing on a t-shirt, I stumbled into the kitchen and grabbed my only knife, then made my way to the front door and looked through the peephole. Lizzy and Jolene stood in the hall, and Lizzy was beating on the door with her fist.

It took me a moment to collect myself enough to open the door and dissolve the ward.

"What's going on? Is the building on fire?"

They barged past me.

"Trevor told us you fought the Hunter last night," Jolene said. "Do you have any coffee?"

"I don't think so," Lizzy's voice came from the kitchen. "She has tea, though." I heard the tap turn on and the sound of my teakettle being filled.

"What time is it?"

"Eight o'clock," Jolene said. "Actually, eight-ten." She looked around the apartment, taking in the complete lack of furniture. "What do you sit on?"

"The bed."

Lizzy came back from the kitchen. "Oh, wow. You don't have any furniture?"

I shook my head. "The apartment was unfurnished. I'm saving to buy some."

"Hell, we can do something about that," Jolene said.

Lizzy nodded, then went back into the kitchen, and I heard the refrigerator open. "No cream?" she called.

"No."

"Do you always greet visitors like that?" Jolene asked, pointing to the knife in my hand.

"I never have visitors, except for the Hunter, and even he doesn't show up at the crack of dawn."

They both laughed.

"We think we know how to find the Hunter," Jolene said. "Lizzy thinks that she can identify where he's living, and if she's right, then I can probably find it."

I went into the kitchen as the teakettle started to whistle and put the knife away. Lizzy poured hot water into three mugs, and said, "Grab one. Let's go where we can sit down."

She picked up two of the mugs and headed back toward the living room. By the time I got there, my visitors were already in my bedroom. They picked different corners of the bed and sat down. I brought a box with a plastic grocery bag that I used as a trash bin and set it near so they could toss their tea bags, then I crawled on the bed, pulling the covers over my legs.

"Did you ask Sam about a trap spell?" Jolene asked.

"I haven't seen Sam. I won't see him until I go into work today."

"Okay," Lizzie said. "We need something from the Hunter. Did you happen to get a scrap of clothing, or even better, some blood or hair from him last night?"

I rolled my eyes. "Hell, no. We're lucky he didn't collect our blood."

They exchanged glances.

"Trevor told us that you knocked him down. Perhaps he dropped something or scraped himself on the ground. Can we go there and check it out?" Lizzy asked.

"It was at a bus stop. Who knows how many people have tromped through there since then."

"Between three o'clock and now? That's a nightlife district," Jolene said. "It's worth a shot. Come on, get dressed."

I took a quick shower and braided my hair, threw on some jeans, a t-shirt, my boots, and we were out the door. I still hadn't had breakfast or anything at all to eat since my meal at work the previous evening.

Lizzy drove us to the bus stop, and we got out of the car. I explained how the fight progressed and showed them where the Hunter had fallen and then the route he used to escape.

My expectation that they would find anything was zero. I couldn't tell them that the Hunter's clothing consisted of skin-tight ballistic cloth, with gloves and a balaclava that covered him from crown to soles with only his eyes exposed. Besides, he was shielded. There wouldn't be any skin or cloth, not even a loose thread.

Lizzy studied the ground where the Hunter had fallen, very slowly scanning every inch of the area. After about five minutes, she pulled a small pair of tweezers and a small plastic bag out of her purse and used the tweezers to pick something up. She dropped it in the bag and held it up.

"You don't wear contacts, do you?" she asked.

"No, I don't."

"This has residual magic," she said, a note of triumph in her voice. I leaned closer to look at what she had, and saw it was a contact lens. It must have jarred loose when I kicked him. Not being attached to him anymore, it would have fallen free of his shield.

After another half an hour searching the area, then following the path of the Hunter's retreat, she announced, "Yup. It's his. I can see the same magic residuals on these twigs." She pointed to the leafless branches of the trees hanging down low enough that someone might have brushed them in passing.

We piled back into her car and drove to Rosie's where I gratefully grabbed a menu as we sat at the bar. I ordered a full Irish breakfast, and then told Sam about Trevor and my adventure earlier that morning and Lizzy's find.

"What we're wondering," I concluded, "is if you know anyone who can cast a trap spell. I can cast a ward that would hold him, but I would have to have him stationary first."

Sam gave us a thoughtful look, then studied the contact lens in the little baggie.

"I can cast a trap spell," he finally said. "And I can teach you how to do it."

"Witch magic?" I asked. I was sure Sam was a mage, not a witch.

He shook his head. "No, it's mage magic, a variation of the ward I have on the door. The way we would do it is, you set up one of those hybrid wards of yours but not trigger it. The trap spell is the trigger, but we need something of his—blood, hair, even a few skin cells—to make it personal to him. I'm not sure there would be enough of his personal DNA or whatever on that lens to do it. Of course, you can set a trap spell that will catch anyone who walks into it, along with mice, pigeons, and roaches, but I doubt that's what you want."

I ate my breakfast, then Jolene and Lizzy took me back to my place. They planned to use the contact lens to try and find the Hunter and told me they would let me know if they had any success.

After washing my hair, I put on my work clothes and went back to Rosie's. Even if I never got the necessary ingredients to trap the Hunter, I wasn't going to let a chance to learn Sam's trap spell go to waste.

The middle of the afternoon was Rosie's slowest time, so we left Liam tending the bar, and Sam took me to the riverside park between the bar and my apartment. There were stretches where there weren't any buildings near the creek, and we found a place where we would be safe from witnesses.

Sam set up a ward using four trees as the anchors, then took a strand of my hair, spelled it, and laid it between two of the trees. He drew on the nearby ley line, twisted the magic into a pattern similar to a Celtic knot, and overlaid that on the strand of hair.

"Okay, walk between the trees, passing over the hair," he directed.

I stepped through the area where he indicated, and

light flashed between the trees. I walked around, feeling with my hands, and found I was completely sealed into the space.

After he dissolved the ward, he gave me a whisker from his sideburns, and I tried it. It took me four tries to get the pattern woven correctly, but when I did, and he stepped into the space between the wards, I was rewarded with a flash of light as the ward closed.

I cast the spell twice more successfully, then we drove back to the bar.

"What happens if you cast that without the hair?" I asked as we drove.

"You'll catch anyone who happens by."

"So, I could hypothetically cast it on my balcony and catch him if he tries to get in that way again."

Sam chuckled. "That would work if he came when you weren't home. Do you want to be trapped in your apartment with him? Keep in mind, that would leave your front door unguarded, unless you set a trigger on that door as well." He thought for a moment, then said, "It seems he's keeping track of your movements. Do you know if he's tried to get in when you aren't home?"

"No. I don't have any way of knowing that."

He lifted his hand off the steering wheel and sketched a rune in the air. It glowed briefly, then faded. "Did you catch that?" he asked.

"Yeah."

"Weave that into the spell when you cast your ward, and it will let you know if someone has tried it."

---

Blair came in after the dinner rush was over and ordered

a beer. When I brought it to him, he handed me a folded piece of paper. Opening it, I found a pencil sketch of a man's face.

"Ever seen him?"

I shook my head.

"The guy you and Frankie took down said that is the man who hired him and his buddies. Dark hair with a hint of salt-and-pepper on the sides, and blue eyes. Said he was in his late forties or early fifties."

I studied the drawing but couldn't remember ever seeing him. "You know, don't you, that a mage could be two or three times that age? We don't age at the same rate normal people do," I said. Master Benedict was well over two hundred and looked to be around sixty. Of course, if I was looking at a picture of the Hunter, he probably was under a hundred. Even mages' reflexes began to slow as they aged.

"You can keep that," Blair said. "Do you like ballet?"

The change of subject took me by surprise. "Yes, I do. I think every little girl has dreams of becoming a ballerina." I had taken ballet classes when I was young, before the Illuminati. After I went to live with them, my classes had changed to the martial arts.

"Sleeping Beauty is going to be performed at the opera house Saturday night," Blair said. "I wondered if you'd like to go."

The smile I gave him probably reflected the hint of sadness I felt. "I would love to, but I have to work." I had seen a video of Sleeping Beauty but never a live performance. The City of the Illuminati didn't have television, but the older Masters were fans of ballet and opera, chamber music and symphonies. I had been to a couple of live performances while on missions. The rich and influential liked to hang out at such cultural events. See and be seen.

"Won't Sam let you switch shifts with someone for one night?"

I shrugged. But as I tended to my other customers, I thought about it.

When I took Blair another beer, I said, "I wouldn't have taken you for a ballet person, Lieutenant."

He smiled. "My mother was a dancer before she married my father. I also have season tickets to the opera."

"Really? Rubbing elbows with all the upper crust?"

With a chuckle, he said, "Yes. As a matter of fact, the mayor's chief of staff has the seats right next to mine this season. All the politicians go to hang out with their rich donors."

"Like Frankie's boss and captains of industry?"

"Yep, those are the ones."

There was more than one way to skin a cat. "Let me talk to Sam. Maybe I can work something out."

Blair beamed, and I felt a little guilty.

I gave Sam a call, and he said he would move the schedule around. One of the other bartenders had asked for some extra shifts, and he said she would gladly fill in for me. When I hung up, I went back to Blair.

"Sam says I can have Saturday off. So, what's the plan?"

"I'll pick you up at your place about five. We'll go to dinner, and then to the ballet."

"Sounds good," I said. But my mind was already swirling with things I would have to do.

For the second morning in a row, someone knocked on my door. I was already awake, however, although just barely. I was in the kitchen making a cup of tea and went to the door to see who it was. I saw Jolene's face through the peephole and opened the door.

I didn't expect the shocked expression on her face, and then I realized I was nude except for my panties.

"Put on some clothes," she said with some urgency. "We have a bunch of guys with us." I noticed that she had a chair sitting on the floor next to her.

I hurried to my bedroom and pulled on a t-shirt and jeans. When I came out, I discovered Josh and another guy who I didn't know maneuvering a sofa through my door. Behind them, Trevor and a fourth guy carried an overstuffed chair. And behind them came Lizzy, carrying another chair, a match for the one Jolene had already put in my kitchen.

The men all trooped out and down the stairs. I walked to the end of the hall and looked through the window overlooking the parking lot. A pickup truck was parked in my space, the back of it filled with furniture.

By the time the truck was empty, I had a sofa and a chair in the living room that didn't match, a coffee table and a side table that didn't match, along with two lamps that didn't match. The dinette set in the kitchen did match, but the night stand and the bureau in my bedroom didn't. I stared at all of it with my mouth hanging open.

"And here's a housewarming present," Lizzy said with a huge smile, handing me a ceramic teapot with an infuser. "Now you can properly entertain guests."

"What—where—?"

"We called around and asked people if they had any old furniture they would like us to haul away for free," Jolene said. "Welcome to Westport."

I looked at the men, who all looked very pleased with themselves, and felt very awkward.

Lizzy whispered in my ear, "Give each of them a hug and a kiss on the cheek."

So I did. It felt kind of weird, but it seemed to please them. In spite of the Hunter and all the other problems I had encountered in Westport, I realized I had friends, for the first time since I was thirteen years old, and it felt pretty damned good.

After brushing my hair and my teeth, I took them all to Rosie's and bought them breakfast with some of the money I was saving for furniture.

## CHAPTER 21

After breakfast, I took the bus to a clothing store and spent the money I had planned to buy a dinette set with on a nice cocktail dress, a pair of pantyhose, a lacy demi bra, a pair of high heels, some make up, a new purse, some curlers, and a couple of pieces of costume jewelry. The bill came to more than I could afford, but I decided I could eat a little less until my next paycheck.

While I wasn't supermodel material, I knew how to present what I had in the best possible way. A good portion of my training had been aimed at placing me in high society settings where I might meet and engage with wealthy and influential men. High society girls weren't all movie-star beautiful—even with expensive surgery—and a lot of what I had learned was attitude, poise, and witty banter. I could fit into upscale social circles and flirt with the best of them when I wanted to. Of course, the Illuminati supplied me with all the necessary money for that, and money wasn't something I could magically conjure. Unfortunately.

There were some things a female Hunter could do that a man couldn't, and the Illuminati never let such petty concerns as ethics and morality interfere with reaching their goals. When it came to staying alive, I wasn't going to let such things get in my way, either.

Daniel Nava, the District Attorney and Frankie's boss, had been a successful prosecutor, gone into private practice and made a bundle, then run for office. Nava was a widower, and his two daughters were at university. Nothing I could find in my or Trevor's research indicated he had a lover or a steady girlfriend, but I did find several pictures on the internet of him with beautiful young women at society events. Never the same woman more than twice.

Charles Mietzner, the mayor's chief of staff, was also single. I couldn't find any evidence he had ever been married, and that added to my suspicions that he might be an Illuminati. His career was as a political operative, and it certainly appeared that he was positioning the mayor for a run for governor in the next election. As with Nava, he rarely appeared at public functions alone and had been linked romantically to several wealthy women, models, and movie starlets over the years, always younger than he was.

When Saturday rolled around, I washed and curled my hair, applied makeup, and dressed. Blair buzzed my apartment promptly at five. I went downstairs, wondering for the first time how Jolene and Lizzy got to the third floor without me letting them in the building.

I opened the door to find Blair dressed in a tailored black suit. He looked very dashing, and I wondered if the suit was bought specifically to attend such events as the opera and ballet.

"Good evening, Lieutenant."

"Whoa!"

I gave him a coy smile. "Is that a good whoa, or a bad whoa?"

"You're beautiful."

"And you're a liar, but a very sweet one. Shall we go?"

He was driving a different car than I'd seen before, a sporty Japanese sedan that appeared to be two or three years old. Not as racy as Frankie's poor destroyed car, nor the kind of flashy German car that men trying to impress women tended to buy.

We drove to a parking garage downtown and walked two blocks to a restaurant called *La Maison*. The maître d seated us quickly, and a waiter greeted Monsieur Blair by name. I glanced at the menu, and the prices.

"Do you come here often?" I asked.

He gave me a disarming grin. "Whenever I attend a performance. It puts me in the mood to mingle with people who spend more on shoes than I make in a month."

"I must admit, Lieutenant, that you are full of surprises."

"Jordan. I'm off duty. And may I call you Erin?"

I grinned. "I'm off duty, too, Jordan."

He ordered wine as we perused the menu. The prices were way above anything I could afford but nowhere near what I had seen in restaurants in New York, Washington, and London. I raised my eyes from the menu, and he caught me looking at him.

"If I couldn't afford this, I would have chosen a cheaper restaurant," he said with a smile. I returned his smile and focused on the halibut, the description of which made my mouth water.

After we ordered, he raised his wine glass. "To the most beautiful woman in Westport."

I felt my face ignite. Refusing to meet his eyes, I said, "That's really not fair." I bit my lip, trying to hold it together. What I wanted to do was jump up and run, but I reminded myself of why I was there.

Blair reached across the table and laid his hand on mine. "I apologize. I didn't mean to make you uncomfortable. I guess what I should have said was that I'm very glad to spend some time alone with you."

His expression was very earnest, and I relaxed a little. I had thought about such a situation while I was getting ready that afternoon. "You don't have to flatter me," I said. "This is very nice, and I'm really looking forward to the ballet. I'd be much more comfortable if we could just think of us as friends—or comrades in arms, perhaps. And let's just see how things work out. Okay?"

"I think I can do that," he said.

"You don't get out enough," I said. "Dealing with corpses all day has to cloud your perspective. You're just excited to see a woman who's still breathing."

He grinned. "You're probably right."

We had a nice dinner, and I was able to steer the conversation away from me and toward him. He had a sailboard and liked to sail on the river on his days off. He also had interests in travel and art. "Although I don't get to travel as much as I'd like to," he said.

After dinner, we strolled down the street to the opera house, which was a couple of blocks away. He led me to seats on the front row of the mezzanine.

"These are incredible seats," I told him when we were seated.

"I was able to get the same seats I have for the opera. With a season subscription, I get first choice for other shows here."

"Two seats? What would you have done if I couldn't come?"

He laughed. "Asked my sister. She never turns me down."

"Then she probably hates me."

"No, she's always telling me I should date more."

His face was calm, relaxed, without the tension I always associated with him.

"Do you always find your dates from the list of current murder suspects?" I asked.

He blushed. "No. And you're not a suspect."

"But I was." And I would never tell him his suspicions were correct as far as that vamp near the bus station.

Blair didn't answer, but his blush deepened.

A few minutes later, just before the performance began, another couple came and sat down beside us. The man who sat next to me was Charles Mietzner, and his companion was a stunning blonde, maybe ten years older than I was.

Mietzner appeared to be around fifty years old, with brown hair and brown eyes. He stood a little short of six feet tall and seemed to be in good shape. He wore a bespoke suit, a diamond tie stud, and a Rolex watch. Everything about him exuded wealth and class.

His magic was palpable. Most mages could feel magic in someone else, but what kind of magic, and how strong, was a difficult thing to determine. In the same way, whether a mage was malevolent or not was impossible to tell. I had my own access to the ley lines choked down to an absolute minimum so as to seal my magic off from detection. Depending on how well he could do that, Mietzner might be very powerful and partially concealing it, or I could be feeling all of his power.

The performance started, and I allowed myself to be swept away in the music and the dancing. But I stayed aware of the fact that I held a portion of Mietzner's attention.

When the intermission came, Blair introduced me, and Mietzner introduced his companion. She was a norm, and from her dress and jewelry, it didn't require a wild guess to figure that she didn't ever worry about paying her rent.

"I'm very pleased to meet you," Mietzner said to me, holding my eyes with his own. "Jordan has been holding out on all of us."

"I'm new in Westport," I said, giving him a thousand-watt smile. "Jordan was kind enough to invite me tonight." I reached out behind me, taking Blair's hand and squeezing it—the kind of gesture meant to reassure him. But all my attention was on Mietzner, and all his attention was on me. His companion didn't look especially pleased.

"Well, welcome to Westport," Mietzner said. "I hope you find our city to your liking, and I hope that I'll see you again."

"I do like it here," I said, "and I'm looking forward to meeting new people and seeing more of the city." I held his eyes with mine, doing everything I could to project an invitation.

During the second part of the ballet, Mietzner leaned close to me and muttered, "I would enjoy learning more about you."

"If I had your phone number, that might be possible," I murmured back. When the performance ended, Mietzner shook my hand as we were saying goodbye, and left a small piece of paper with a phone number in my palm. His touch was almost electric. The man was definitely plugged into the ley line.

I put my arm through Blair's while we walked back to his car. He seemed happy, and when he walked me to the door of my apartment building, I leaned forward and kissed him on the cheek.

"I had a wonderful time tonight. Thank you so much for inviting me."

"Perhaps we can do it again," he said.

"I would like that." I used my key and entered my building, climbed the stairs, and reached my apartment. My wards were still in place, but sitting in the hall in front of my door was a head. A vampire's head. She was blonde and macabrely grinning at me.

I whirled, casting a personal shield, but I was alone in the hallway. Not sure what to do, I cautiously made my way back downstairs, expecting to encounter the Hunter at any moment. To say I was freaked out would be a massive understatement.

I couldn't see anyone in the parking lot, so I took off my heels and set them by the door. Opening it, I sprinted across the short distance to the office where Eleanor's apartment was. I could see a light on in one of her windows. There was an emergency button next to the office door. I pushed on it and let it buzz, not caring if that was rude.

"What is it?" the box next to the buzzer asked.

"It's Erin! It's an emergency. Let me in!"

The door buzzed, I pulled it open, jumped inside, and pulled the door shut behind me.

"What is the matter?" Eleanor's voice said from behind me.

I whirled around and said, "There's a vampire's head sitting in the hallway in front of my door."

She didn't waste any time, rushing behind the counter and picking up the phone. I could tell from her end of the conversation that she didn't call the police, and that was confirmed about ten minutes later when Sam's SUV pulled into the parking lot.

He came to the door, and Eleanor buzzed him in.

"Are you all right?" he asked, looking back and forth between Eleanor and me. We both nodded, and he gave me his full attention.

"You sure clean up damned good," he said. "Now, what happened?"

"There's a head in front of my door. A vampire's head." Even to my own ears I sounded a little shrill. I gulped some air and tried to calm down. I knew meditation exercises to calm myself, but practicing that sort of thing and actually doing it when confronted with someone's bloody head were two different things.

"I tell people not to do that," Eleanor said.

"Do what?" My voice rose almost to a shriek.

"Buzz people in if they don't know them. People, salesmen mostly, will press all the buttons hoping someone will let them in without checking to see if it's someone they know."

More vehicles pulled into the parking lot. I

recognized some of the people getting out of them as regulars at the bar. Others I had never seen.

"Well, let's go see," Sam said.

We waited for Eleanor to get some shoes on, then went outside. Sam held a brief conversation with the people outside, and a number of them fanned out, some going around my building and others checking out the area around the other buildings.

I led a small group to my apartment. Sam was huffing a bit by the time we reached the third floor.

He walked up to the head and lifted it by the hair, revealing a black stain on the carpet.

"Not much blood," Sam said. "Looks like she was killed somewhere else and bled out before he brought her here." He sounded so matter-of-fact. Maybe that was good, because I was freaking out and his manner calmed me down a little bit.

"Are your wards still intact?" he asked.

"Yeah."

"Open up," he said. "I want to make sure there aren't any surprises."

I stepped around the black stain and opened the door. Sam started to follow me in, and I said, "You're not bringing that thing in here."

He looked at the head in his hand as though he'd forgotten he was carrying it, then carefully set it down on the black spot.

Sam and Eleanor followed me into the apartment and watched as I checked the place out. I even looked under the bed.

"No, as far as I can tell, no one has been in here."

"What are you going to do with that?" Eleanor asked Sam, indicating the head.

"Give it to Blair. Where do you want me to tell him I found it?" he asked me.

"Not here."

He nodded. "I'll tell him I found it at Rosie's. Close enough to the truth."

I got a trash bag and he deposited the head in it.

Sam looked pointedly at the stain, and Eleanor said, "Don't worry about that. I'll take care of it in the morning."

I reset my wards, and we trooped back downstairs where I retrieved my shoes.

The people who had deployed around the apartment complex trickled back and reported they hadn't found anything or anyone suspicious. Soon, everyone got back in their vehicles and drove off. I went back upstairs to my apartment, stepping gingerly around the black stain.

I poured myself a double shot of whiskey, then undressed, put my clothes away, washed my face, and went to bed. It took a long time to fall asleep, and the dreams weren't good. In one, a Hunter with the vampire's head chased me around my apartment.

## CHAPTER 22

I had told Lizzy and Jolene that I was going out with Blair, and they showed up at my place about ten o'clock in the morning.

When I opened the door, I looked at the floor. Eleanor obviously got up earlier than I did, and whatever spell she used on the carpet did the trick, because there wasn't a trace of vampire blood.

"Let's go to brunch," Lizzy said, "and you can tell us all about your hot date."

They took me to a restaurant overlooking the ocean, bright and open, with all-you-can-drink mimosas and a fantastic buffet. How they managed to land a table next to a window, I didn't know, but the view was great. It was a rare bright and sunny day, with sailboats out on the water and gulls flying overhead. The sun sparkled on the whitecaps and the windows of the houses on the islands dotting the bay.

"So, spill," Jolene said. "How was the ballet?"

"And how was Lieutenant Dreamy?" Lizzy asked. "Did you kiss him?"

My face flamed, and they both laughed.

"Are you going out again?" Jolene asked.

"Maybe. He has season tickets to the opera."

"Ooo," Jolene said. "A mutual interest in opera. Must be serious."

I shook my head. "I don't think so. I mean, I don't know what love is supposed to feel like, but I don't get all hot and bothered when I'm with him. Aren't you supposed to do that when you're in love?"

I told them about dinner and the ballet. They sobered when I described meeting Mietzner. Then I told them about the head, and their shock was obvious.

"Oh my God," Jolene breathed. "Well, obviously you can't meet with Mietzner. That's far too dangerous. I mean, if he's the guy who called in the Hunter, then he's the one who's trying to kill you."

"I wouldn't go alone," I said. "I'll arrange some kind of backup."

That got me a couple of very skeptical looks. To change the subject, I pulled out the sketch Blair had given me. "This is the guy who hired the thugs who attacked Frankie. Is there any way you can use this?"

They both leaned forward, studying the sketch.

"Police artist?" Jolene asked.

"Yeah."

Lizzy's eyes seemed to cloud, and her face lost all expression. She sat like that, staring at the picture, for about five minutes. During that time, Jolene sat back and sipped at her mimosa, casually looking out over the view outside.

Eventually, Lizzy leaned back in her chair, her eyes cleared, and she reached for her glass.

"Anything?" Jolene asked.

"Maybe," Lizzy said. "Possibly. I think I can feed you something to fuel a finding spell. Whether we come up with anything…" She shrugged.

---

Jill, the late-night bartender, came in an hour early that night. She ate dinner at the bar and we chatted. She was interested in hearing more about the vampire riot in the alley, and she laughed when I told her I had waded in using Sam's magical bat.

"Yeah, I've only had to haul that thing out twice in all the time I've worked here," she said. "I had a troll come in one night, and after he drank a couple of bottles of whiskey, he decided to bust up the place. I kneecapped him with than bat, and he went down like a chopped tree."

"Do you get many Fae on your shift?" I asked. I had never seen one of the Fae in the bar.

"Every so often," she replied. "They mostly hang out in Killarney, but once in a while, I'll have one or two stop by. But that was the only troll. I think word got around that this wasn't the place for them to go."

Steve Dworkin and I left Rosie's after our shift that night and were immediately jumped by at least a dozen vampires. I followed Steve out the door and didn't have time to react before one of them shoved a gun against my head and pushed me face-first against the wall. Out of the corner of my eye, I saw Steve pressed against the wall and a vampire holding a pistol barrel against the back of his head.

"Don't move, and no one will get hurt," a voice said. "Now, girlie, you're going to walk, and be a good girl, or we'll blow your boyfriend's head off. Understand?"

"Yes," I managed to say through gritted teeth. I was hyper aware that all it took was a jitter by some idiot and my brains would be splattered all over the alley. A fair fight was one thing, but that gun grinding into my skin about made me wet my pants.

My captor grabbed my coat at the shoulder and pulled me away from the wall, then directed me down the alley toward a waiting black car with its back door open. The gun never wavered, pressing firmly against my head. That didn't stop me from pulling power from the ley line.

When we reached the car, the vampire released me and pushed me into the back seat. The pressure of the gun on my head disappeared, and I felt the barrel catch in my hair, then he pulled the gun away, trying to disentangle it.

I kicked backward and heard bone snap. The gun went off over my head, then I whirled and drove my fist into his throat. My other hand closed over his wrist and crushed his bones. He dropped the gun, and I snatched it up as I took off running, casting my shield as I did so. I hoped my escape didn't put Steve in more danger. Hopefully, the distraction might give him a chance to escape, too. But I wasn't about to get in that car if I could help it. I had visions of the cops pulling my body out of the river the next day.

A bullet hit my shield, while another hit the wall of the building next to me, and a third ricocheted off the sidewalk. When I reached the next street, I stuck out my hand and used the building to help me swing around the corner without losing much momentum.

Vampires are supernaturally fast, so I had no hope of outrunning them. All I wanted was to reach a place where I could turn and fight without any witnesses. Between Rosie's and my apartment complex was a lot of open land—a park, several vacant lots, and an old flour mill that had been closed for decades, a crumbling ruin with a chain link fence surrounding it.

I stuck the pistol in my purse and drew the purse strap over my head. I couldn't use the pistol with my shield in place, but I didn't want to lose it.

One of the vampires caught up with me, suddenly running beside me and grinning at me. He thought he'd won the game. I cast a glance over my shoulder and didn't see any more of them who were close.

I reached out and grabbed his arm, then sent a jolt of energy into him. His arm buckled in an unnatural way, and he flew from me, landing about twenty feet away and rolling along the ground. I kept running.

Two more vampires caught up with me as I reached the park, flanking me, and then trying to get in front of me. I assumed more of their friends were right behind.

As soon as they got close enough, I gave both of them a blast of energy that sent them tumbling.

My morning runs were something I dreaded. Some people got off on the endorphins and enjoyed that kind of exercise. I did it out of habit and the dread that I might fall out of shape. That night, I was glad I had kept up the practice. Vampires had a lot of supernatural abilities, but they couldn't expend energy at a high rate forever. I had never heard of a vampire exercising regularly. They didn't chase their prey but were ambush predators.

I reached the old flour mill and scrambled over the

fence. The closest vamps were a couple of hundred yards behind me.

Working my way through the debris and junk, I found a wide, open area surrounded by buildings, with the storage towers to my back. Making sure I had good footing in the area, I waited for the vampires to find me.

In discussions with Sam and some of the other people I knew, I downplayed my magical talents. While I couldn't throw fireballs or orange balls of energy or spin mini-tornadoes out of thin air, I did have a couple of lethal abilities up my sleeve. The spot I'd chosen to make my stand was ideal primarily because there couldn't be any witnesses.

Three vampires appeared out of the shadows, creeping closer to me, fanning out to cut off any escape. I waited.

As soon as all three were in range, I extended my hand, palm out, and pushed three green balls of energy, a little smaller than a baseball, one at each of the vamps. Pure, unfiltered ley line energy that my Masters had called ley missiles. The balls hit the vamps and vaporized them. No sound, nothing left, just like the Illuminati City after it burned.

Since I had never heard of anyone else creating such a weapon, and the Masters of the Illuminati had never heard of such a weapon, I had always been counseled to be discreet with it. Master Benedict and I had done some limited experimentation with the power, but I still wasn't sure exactly what I could do with it. I did know that if I missed one of the vamps, the ball would fizzle out past a certain distance. If it hit something before it traveled that distance, it would blow a big-ass hole in whatever it hit. There would be no sound and no debris.

I had never tried to use that power against a shielded mage and had no idea what would happen if I did. In fact, the only time I'd used it in a real fight was against the Austrian vampire lord.

Two more vamps found me about five minutes later and then disappeared from the face of the earth shortly thereafter.

I waited another half an hour, then heard shouting and a muffled explosion coming from the direction I had entered the old mill grounds. Cautiously making my way in that direction, I peered out from behind a building and saw several mages engaged with a group of vampires on the other side of the fence. Farther away, at the main road, a number of cars and trucks were parked. The faint sound of sirens could be heard in the distance.

A fireball illuminated the scene, and a vampire exploded in fire, keening his last farewell to life. As the fireball left the mage's hand, I could see it was Steve Dworkin, and I breathed a sigh of relief.

In short order, the vampires broke and ran, chased by fireballs and energy bolts. Some of the cars out by the road started their engines, then pulled away.

I climbed over the fence and found Steve.

"Thank the gods you're okay," he said, pulling me into a hug that almost crushed me.

"Yeah, I managed to outrun them and hide in there," I said, pointing to the mill. "I'm just glad you're all right. I was afraid they might hurt you when I escaped."

He chuckled. "Your escape and the guy shooting at you distracted the guy holding me. So, I combusted."

He grinned. "As you can see, I survived the experience much better than he did."

We walked back to where the remaining cars were parked, and I recognized my rescuers as regulars who had been drinking or eating at the bar when Steve and I left. He told me that he had gone back inside and put together a posse to ride to my rescue. I made sure to memorize each of their faces. I owed quite a few free drinks. A lot of my tips were going to saying thank you instead of feeding me.

Sam pulled up about that time and demanded to know what had happened. Everyone had to tell him, so it was quite some time before he told me to get in his SUV and he drove me home.

"Any idea who they were?" Sam asked me.

"Barclay's men," I said. "I recognized a couple of them from when we were out at his mansion. Or at least I think so. Flynn seems to know an awful lot of what's going on at Barclay's mansion. And since it seems Barclay doesn't really control the mansion, or the city, how would an outsider know what the allegiances are?"

"Remember that Columbia Club thing you were telling me about?" Sam asked.

"Yeah?"

"Were Ronald Jenkins or Everitt Johnson members?"

"They both were. Why?"

The grim look on Sam's face got even grimmer. "Both of them were murdered this week. The cops think Jenkins was mugged in the parking garage under his office building. Beaten to death. Johnson was stabbed on the street near his office in downtown. How about Brian Douglas?"

"Yeah, he's a member." Douglas was a city councilman.

"He died last week. They say it was a heart attack, but he was only fifty-two and didn't have any previous history."

I took a deep breath. "You know, I suspect that whoever brought in the Hunter plans a power grab. Were all of those men backers of our current mayor?"

Sam snorted. "Just the opposite. Douglas was his leading opponent on the Council."

"I think it's started. Sam, I think that either Daniel Nava or Charles Mietzner are responsible for bringing in the Hunter."

We drove on in silence, but when he pulled up in front of my apartment building, he turned off the engine and twisted to face me.

"What aren't you telling me? For a girl as young as you are, you seem to know a helluva lot about politics, Hunters, and how things work behind the scenes. Erin, if you want me to trust you, you have to trust me. I've backed you every step of the way since you walked into my bar. I've put my life on the line and asked others to do the same for you. But I need to understand why I should continue to do that instead of just kicking you out and solving one of my biggest problems."

I sat there, staring down at my hands. He was right, of course. But if even one person knew, would that sacrifice my safety? A voice in the back of my mind said, *what safety?*

Taking a deep breath, I said, "I'm afraid to tell you, because if anyone knew about me, I'd probably be dead in a week."

"So, you're not going to trust me."

I looked up into his face and made a decision.

"I was a Hunter. The Illuminati are real. And no one leaves them and lives."

His eyes flicked over me, taking in my body and then focusing on my face. "A Hunter. Training to be a Hunter?"

I shook my head. Unable to meet his eyes, I bowed my head and looked down at my lap. "I formally entered the Hunters' Guild and took my first assignment when I was nineteen. I've killed more than two hundred people on orders from the Illuminati. I killed five vampires tonight. Unarmed. If I had my sword, I wouldn't have needed any help to kill them all."

"Where is your sword?"

"Gone. Destroyed along with the rest of my weapons. I left that life behind me."

He sat back and surveyed me in silence. Then he said, "Did you grow up with them?"

"From when I was fourteen. The power storm that came when I hit puberty almost killed me. My parents went looking for help, and someone contacted one of the Illuminati. They came and tested me, then they gave my parents some money and took me away. I didn't see the outside world again until I was eighteen, when they took me outside as part of my training."

He shook his head. "Well, that explains a lot. On the one hand, you're one of the toughest, smartest women I know. And sometimes you act like a naïve little girl on her first trip to the store by herself. I guess you're both of those."

I felt a tear roll down my cheek. "I'm just trying to do the best I can. I watch people to try and figure out the everyday things that everyone seems to know.

Cooking is a lot harder than it looks." I glanced at him, trying to read his face. "People give me weird looks sometimes when I ask questions."

Taking a deep breath, I looked back down at my hands and closed my eyes. I didn't want to say it, but I knew I had to.

"I did so many bad things, and when I found out what the Illuminati really was, how evil and corrupt they were, I didn't know what to do. When I found out that I'm a monster, I struggled with whether to kill myself. Do you know how hard it is to admit you've done horrendous things? That you're an evil person?" I shook my head. "But I didn't. I judged myself and decided I could put it behind me."

I opened my eyes and looked at Sam. "Fuck anyone who thinks they have the right to judge me. I'm really trying to be a good person, and sometimes I'm not sure how to do that. What I do know is that I'll never let anyone else decide right and wrong for me ever again. And anyone who tries to hurt me had better watch their ass, because I'll fight to be left alone and live my life."

After a moment, Sam got out of the truck. I watched him walk around, and then open my door. I cringed. He pulled me out, but instead of throwing me away like I expected, he folded me into a hug. Stars and comets, the man was huge, and it felt like being enveloped by a feather bed.

The dam broke. All my emotions, everything I had bottled up from the moment I killed William Strickland burst out. The fear, the rage, the feeling of being utterly alone in the world. Everyone had a place but me. I found myself clinging to Sam and sobbing. Something in the back of my mind shouted, *Hunters don't cry!* And I shouted back, *Shut up! I'm not a Hunter anymore!*

I don't know how long we stood there, with me crying on his shirt and him patting me on the back. But finally, there weren't any more tears to shed, and the aching pain inside me faded a bit. I looked up at him, and all I saw in his face was kindness.

"You're pretty damned naïve yourself," I mumbled, "falling for that old crying female trick."

"Ah, yes," he said with a chuckle. "I've always been a sucker for that one. Old Softie, they call me."

He bent down and kissed me on the forehead. "Come on. I'll walk you inside in case your old comrade left you another present."

We didn't find a head, or anything else out of place. After I unlocked my door and assured Sam that I didn't have any visitors, he wished me good night.

And for some reason, I felt lighter. My sleep was untroubled by dreams.

## CHAPTER 23

F rankie called Eleanor, who came to my apartment. "Assistant District Attorney Francis Jones asked you to call her," Eleanor said, handing me a piece of paper with a phone number. "If you need to use the phone, come by the office."

I showered and got dressed, then went down to the office.

"Thanks for calling, Erin," Frankie said. "Can you please come downtown to my office? I need a formal statement from you so I can file an insurance claim for my car."

"Oh? What do you want me to say?" The thought of telling the insurance company about magic amused me.

"Just what happened. My car was parked in front of your building, and when we came out, we found it on fire. They're trying to say I must have done something to make it burn. Essentially accusing me of insurance fraud."

"Well, that is what happened," I said with a chuckle.

"I also would like to talk with you about some other things," she said. That sounded ominous.

So, I took the bus to the train and rode it downtown. It took me a little bit of time, getting lost twice, to find her office. I found the DA's office rather easily in the courthouse, but Frankie's office wasn't on the fifth floor with the other assistant DAs. Nor was it in the basement with Blair's crew. Instead, she was located in the back corner of the building on the third floor.

The receptionist was a witch. The tall, blonde woman who came to get me and take me back through the labyrinth was a mage. We passed the cubicles of several more mages and witches. I got the feeling that Frankie's hiring process was a bit biased.

Frankie stood when I was shown into her office and shook my hand. The assistant stayed, shutting the door.

"Thank you so much for coming," Frankie said. "If you can just read the statement you gave me over the phone, and sign it if it's correct, we can get this bureaucratic irritation out of the way."

I grinned at her. Basically, the statement said that we found the car burning when we went outside and had no idea what caused the fire. I signed it and handed it to her.

"I'll bet it was a disgruntled criminal," I said. "If you stopped prosecuting people, you'd be more popular."

Frankie and her assistant chuckled.

"Erin, this is Debbie McCauley, my chief investigator. We received a disturbing report about a mage battle near the old flour mill on Sloman's Creek last night. Would you know anything about that?"

I considered my answer. I was pretty sure Frankie wasn't my enemy. "Some vampires tried to kidnap me. A

215

few good Samaritans objected." I shrugged. "It was dark. I didn't really get a good look at anyone involved."

McCauley snorted.

"Any idea why they would want to kidnap you?" Frankie asked.

"Any idea why three magical thugs would want to kill you?" I replied.

"Touché. No, I don't. I also don't know why several prominent mages here in town have suffered violent deaths in the past couple of weeks. Those were subtler attacks than the one on me."

"I heard about that," I said.

"You told me once that someone was stirring the pot," Frankie said, "trying to take advantage of the chaos in the paranormal communities." She leaned forward. "I asked you once about the Order of the Illuminati. Most people think they're a myth, but certain people in law enforcement and intelligence have heard rumors about the Order for some time. And this kind of thing is exactly what they seem to foment. Assassination and disruption aimed at furthering their own aims and removing those who might oppose them."

"I wouldn't know anything about the Illuminati," I said, "but removing a Master of the City is, as far as I know, unprecedented. Vampires have a very structured society. You used the word chaos. I'm sure that is how the vampires in this city view things at the moment. There's nothing they can rely on—no stability."

I actually had a lot of sympathy for the vamps. Struggling with a lack of structure and stability, trying to figure out how they fit into the world was something I could relate to. I wondered if there were counselors for young castaway vamps and if they took ex-Illuminati patients.

A knock sounded at the door, and McCauley went to answer it. A man walked in, and I recognized him from his pictures. Daniel Nava, District Attorney. He was of medium height, with an athletic build, brown skin, and slicked-back black hair.

"Sorry to interrupt," he said, "but I heard that Miss McLane was here, and I wanted to meet her."

Jones and McCauley exchanged a look.

I stood and he shook my hand. "I want to thank you for the assistance you gave Assistant DA Jones. The city of Westport is in your debt."

Nava didn't leer at me the way Mietzner had, his expression more that of a benevolent grandfather. He made small talk for a while, mentioned that he used to spend time at Rosie's when he was younger, and asked me how I liked working there. I had seen politicians operate, and Nava was good at it. He was definitely a mage, but either he shielded better, or he was weaker than Mietzner.

When he left, I talked with Frankie and McCauley for a few more minutes, then they let me go. I grabbed lunch before I got back on the train and went home to change for work.

---

George Flynn came into the bar and slid onto a barstool near the taps.

"Good evening. Macallan?" I asked.

He studied the top shelf, then said, "How about Midleton? I haven't had any Irish whiskey in ages."

"I enjoy serving a man with taste," I said.

"You're a Midleton fan?"

I laughed. "I think one has to have the means to afford something in order to be a fan."

I dragged the stool over so I could reach the bottle and climbed up to get it.

"Will you join me?" Flynn asked.

I jerked around so quickly I almost fell off the stool. People buy bartenders shots all the time. The trick normally is to minimize the number of those occasions. But they rarely offered to buy me top-shelf liquor.

"You mean…" I gestured with the bottle as I brought it down.

"Absolutely."

I poured two drinks and set them on the bar. "Sixty dollars."

He handed me a hundred, and after I handed him his change, he held up his glass. I clinked mine against it.

"To the prettiest bartender in town," Flynn said.

I laughed and took a sip of the whiskey. So smooth. I vowed right then and there I would buy a bottle for myself in celebration if I managed to reach my first anniversary at Rosie's.

"I don't have to ask if you say that to every bartender in town," I told him. "It rolls off your tongue too easily. But this is the wrong bar, Mr. Flynn. We're used to Irishmen's blarney in here."

He winked at me, then said, "I heard you had a problem with some of my clansmen last night."

"Are you and Mr. Barclay members of the same clan?"

Flynn shrugged. "So to speak. Nasty business. You know that poor Rodrick isn't quite right, don't you?"

"I'm sorry to hear that. I did notice that he had a terrible pallor."

Flynn choked on his whiskey. When he got his coughing under control, he said, "Ms. McLane, you are delightful. I would enjoy spending eternity with you."

"I seriously doubt that," I said, taking another sip of my drink and moving away to take care of other customers.

When I wandered back after about fifteen minutes, I said, "You seem to have excellent sources of information."

"Barclay doesn't own Carleton House, and although he wants to think of himself as Master of the City, he isn't." Flynn toasted me with his glass and took a sip. "So, he doesn't know who comes and goes there any more than anyone else."

"Do your excellent sources have a clue as to why he attempted to kidnap me?"

"Information has value. What are you willing to trade?"

"I'll take you to lunch tomorrow? *La Maison* at noon?" I said with a hopeful note in my voice.

Flynn laughed. "Oh, Ms. McLane. You'll be magnificent in a hundred years."

"Yes, I will be, and you'll still be striking. Consider my future good will for that hundred years as a great bargain."

He regarded me over the rim of his glass, then said, "I'll take that. Someone in City Hall asked Rodrick to do it."

"Name?"

"Sorry, I'm afraid I don't have that. It seems this person has promised to back him for Master of the City."

"Is that person a vampire?"

Flynn shook his head. "I don't believe so."

"Then how would he be able to help Barclay?" I couldn't imagine how a non-vampire could possibly do that.

"I told you Rodrick isn't quite right."

As far as I was able to determine, four children of Lord Carleton had the age to contend for supremacy, with Flynn and Barclay the strongest contenders. Eventually, one of them would kill the other and ascend the throne. Outsiders normally had very little influence over that struggle.

"Mr. Flynn? Watch your back. I believe that someone in City Hall is directing the Hunter that's in town."

He raised an eyebrow, finished his whiskey, and as he got to his feet, said, "Ms. McLane, that nugget of information was worth a lot more than lunch. Until next time." He smiled, collected his bodyguards, and walked out of the bar.

Sam dropped in later that evening, and I told him about Mietzner and my conversation with Flynn.

"I agree with Lizzy and Jolene," Sam said. "Meeting with Mietzner is too dangerous. I don't care if you do have backup. You said yourself that he's a powerful mage. Too much can go wrong, especially if his backup is the Hunter."

I hadn't thought about that. The Hunter would definitely cancel me out, and I wouldn't be armed. I had the spells in the Book to forge a sword, but I would have to find a skilled metalsmith, possibly through Lizzy's Fae connections, and it would take time. Assuming I could find a Fae smith willing to work with iron. It would be expensive, too. I would probably have to give the smith the spells to pay for it.

I answered the phone around midnight, and Jolene said, "Can you come by my place around noon tomorrow? Lizzy and I are going to try and find your Hunter. Lizzy said she can pick you up at your place around eleven-thirty."

"I'll be there," I said.

And with that to look forward to, sleep didn't come easily when I got home. My mind just wouldn't stop.

## CHAPTER 24

"Trevor did some research for us," Jolene said when Lizzy and I showed up at her house the following day. "Mietzner owns a couple of rental properties. I thought we could cruise by them and see if we can learn anything."

"If we could get anything personal of the Hunter's to focus on, it would make finding him a lot easier," Lizzy said. "Jolene says she can fashion a tracker we might plant on him."

It seemed to me that if we found where he was staying, we wouldn't need a finder spell, but I didn't say anything. If Trevor had given me the information, I would have checked it out. At least with Jolene's and Lizzy's help, I would have transportation.

We took Jolene's car because it was less remarkable. Lizzy's pink Cooper with flower decals was rather noticeable.

The first place we checked was a six-story apartment building downtown. We drove around it, then I asked

Jolene to let me out. Lizzy came with me. There weren't any balconies, and when we walked into the lobby, we discovered there weren't any apartments on the ground floor—just the lobby, a small liquor store with fancy wines, a gym, and a laundry room. There were two sets of stairs and two central elevators.

Shaking my head, I said, "Nope. He wouldn't be here," and walked back out.

"Why do you say that?" Lizzy asked as we stood on the curb waiting for Jolene to come around and pick us up."

"No escape routes. Hard to secure. Not private enough."

She nodded, then shrugged.

Jolene next drove us out to an area near my place. Rather than apartments, the neighborhood was comprised of one-story duplexes with small front yards and walled backyards. According to property tax records, Mietzner owned two buildings—four apartments—right next to each other.

Jolene parked a block away and said, "Hand me that clipboard on the back seat." Lizzy handed it to her, and Jolene got out of the car. "I'll be back in a few minutes."

Fifteen minutes later, she opened the door, tossed the clipboard into the backseat, and got back in the car.

"Nope. No paranormal assassins in residence."

"What did you do?" I had been bursting with curiosity the whole time she had been gone.

"There's a senior center two blocks from here. I rang the bell and said I was doing a survey for the community center. Asked them what services they used, and what programs they would like to see offered. Talked to people in all four addresses, and the youngest one was a woman in her seventies."

We next drove across the river and into a forested area at the base of the foothills. Custom homes on large lots, shielded for the most part from their neighbors and the road by trees. Mietzner's house was on one edge of the neighborhood with trees all around it, and a forested hill rising behind it.

"Trevor said this is where Mietzner lived for a long time, but he built a new house a few years ago. He's been renting this one because the housing market was down."

"This one's going to be a little trickier to scout," I said. "If I was staying here, I'd set wards, but I'd also set some booby traps. Not the kind that would hurt anyone, but that would tell me if someone was sneaking around."

"Yeah," Jolene said. "You either have to sneak through the woods or walk right up the driveway in plain sight of the house. Hard to be discreet. Hand me the clipboard."

Lizzy snorted. "You think people in this neighborhood use senior centers?"

"No, I want to write down the license number on the car in the driveway."

"Let's go grab some lunch and bring it back," I said. "We can go to that fast-food joint we passed. Maybe we can see someone coming out of the house."

I watched for the car while we ordered burgers and fries but didn't see anyone drive by. We got our food and parked down the street where we could see the car but none of the windows in the house. Jolene called Trevor and asked him to check on the car's license number, and then we waited.

After an hour, Trevor called back. Jolene talked to him, taking notes, then asked, "Did you get the name on the credit card?" She wrote some more, then said, "Thanks," and hung up.

Turning to us, she said, "It's a rental car, and it was rented two months ago. The credit card he used is in the name of Hans Christian."

I snorted, and Lizzy asked about silver skates.

"Yeah," Jolene said, "but Trevor hacked the credit card company, and he's got all the places the card was used over the past two months. Restaurants, laundry, gas stations. We can map out a pattern."

We watched for another two hours, and everyone was starting to get fidgety, when a man came out of the house and got in the car. Jolene handed me her binoculars.

"That's the guy from the police sketch," I said, and handed the binoculars to Lizzy.

We watched Christian drive away, and Lizzy jumped out of the car.

"Hey, where are you going?" I called.

"Spell material," she said, trotting away.

"Watch out for booby traps."

Lizzy laughed.

She came back about ten minutes later and jumped into the car.

"You were right," she said. "The house is warded, and there are both magical and physical tripwires set around the place. I think you could get blown up if you weren't careful."

"Physical tripwires?" I asked. "How did you spot those?"

"He tried to hide them with magic, and I can see the magic," she said with a grin.

"Hell. If I ever break into a wizard's castle, you're the first person I'm hiring."

"Did you get anything?" Jolene asked.

Lizzy held up a black glove—a Hunter's glove. I gasped.

"He evidently dropped it and accidently kicked it under a bush, I guess," Lizzy said.

"That's perfect," Jolene said. "Don't turn it inside out until I can get it home."

It was one of my nights off, so we all went to Jolene's.

---

Jolene ordered a pizza, which I thought was pretty neat and made a note to remember I could do that if I ever got a phone.

Lizzy gave Jolene the glove, and she took it out to her lab in the garage. She put on rubber gloves, then turned the glove inside out on a black cloth. Using the back of a knife, she gently scraped the glove, then moved the cloth to a counter near the stove.

"Did I get anything, Lizzy?" Jolene asked.

"Yeah. There's residual magic on the cloth. I think you also got some skin cells."

"Fantastic."

I watched all of that but was puzzled. "I don't understand. We already found him. Why do we need a finding spell?"

Jolene stopped what she was doing and turned to me. "I'm not doing a finding spell. I'm going to create a couple of trackers. One for his car, and one for him. I don't know how we're going to get the one on him, but if we can, we can follow him anywhere."

Lizzy chuckled. "Put it on the glove, then I'll put the glove back somewhere he'll find it." She cocked her head at me, as if asking whether that would work.

"Yeah, that will do it," I said. "That glove is ballistic cloth and leather, with hardened leather over the knuckles and wrists. He's not going to get one like it at the local store."

Jolene gave me a strange look, but Lizzy just looked smug, and I realized I shouldn't have known about the glove, since I'd never handled it.

I watched as Jolene put various liquids in a pot along with a few sprigs of vegetation and heated it. She then took a dot of cloth the size of my thumbnail and dipped it in the mixture. Holding it with a pair of tweezers, she laid it on a button sort of thing she took out of a cabinet, and then put the whole thing on a pedestal at the center of her pentagram.

Next, she put the black cloth in the pot and simmered it for a few minutes. She pulled the cloth out of the pot and laid it on the counter. Passing her hand over the cloth, she mumbled a few words. The cloth looked different, and I leaned closer.

"Touch it," Jolene said. I did and discovered the cloth was dry.

She cut another dot out of the cloth and put it next to the button on the pedestal. Then she pulled two small mirrors out of another cabinet, and with a pair of tweezers, placed each cloth dot on a mirror, then put them on the pedestal.

Her doorbell rang.

"Pizza's here!" Lizzy called out.

"Yeah, I can finish the spell after we eat. I'm starving," Jolene said.

We sat around her kitchen table and ate the pizza, which had different stuff on it than what Trevor had ordered. Jolene laid out her plan. We would plant one of the trackers she was preparing on the Hunter's car. The other she would embed in his glove, then we'd plant the glove back in his driveway and hope he found it. The little mirrors were the receivers.

We trooped back into the garage, where Jolene lit the candles, sprinkled salt around the outline of the circle, and then stepped inside it. She chanted an incantation in a language I didn't know, and then there was a small flash of light from the top of the pedestal. She put one of the trackers in a little plastic bag, then pressed the other against the back of the glove near the wrist and said a Word. Then she scuffed the salt to break the circle and blew out the candles.

"We'll take the glove back out to his house, and then take you home," Jolene said. "We can start trying to track him tomorrow, but I'm bushed."

She gave me a few pages of paper. "These are Hans's credit card charges that Trevor sent me. Go over them and figure out a good place to find him tomorrow so we can plant the tracker on his car."

We drove back out to the Hunter's house. His car wasn't in the driveway, so Lizzy took the glove up to the house.

"I put it right at the base of the front steps," she said

when she returned. You wouldn't see it at night because it will be in shadow, and you don't notice it when you come down the steps from the porch."

Jolene drove to my place, where Lizzy had left her car, and we said good night.

# CHAPTER 25

I went through the credit card charges Trevor provided and marked them on my city map. Then I put together a matrix that showed where he used the card versus the day and time he used it. When I sat back and looked at it, I realized that the Hunter had a favorite place for brunch. He had eaten at the same place and paid his check between ten-thirty and eleven in the morning almost every day for the past five weeks, with only three breaks in the pattern.

Catching him when he wasn't armed—or at least not armed with his sword—had its attraction, but a magical battle in public that ended in one or more people's deaths wasn't something anyone in the shadow world wanted. Frankie would have a huge task in trying to explain away people throwing fireballs in the middle of the city at noon. I tagged the breakfast place as a good place to plant the tracker on his car.

For dinner, he had five places with more than one charge. Most senior Hunters, including me, had unlimited expense accounts. No one cared whether we ate hamburgers or lobster. The Illuminati were so wealthy that even the Masters in charge of their finances didn't know how much money they had. I'd seen their reports on Master Benedict's desk.

Hans Christian was fond of steak and seafood and barbeque. He had been to *La Maison* twice. Considering what I saw of their menu, I would have haunted the place if I had the money. But steaks bigger than my head had never been my thing.

Lizzy came by in the morning. When I got in her car, she said, "I'm going to drop you at Jolene's, and then I have to go to class. I'll hook up with you guys this afternoon."

"I can take the train downtown," I said.

"You don't mind?"

"Not at all. Just drop me at the train station."

Waiting on the platform, I noticed a guy checking me out. Maybe thirty, good-looking, in a millennial-punk sort of way. He wasn't being obnoxious or leering, so I didn't think too much about it.

He changed trains when I did and got off at the same station. Several other people did as well. I thought I might have seen one of the women around my apartment complex. My hours were so weird that I hadn't met many of my neighbors.

I stopped in at a convenience store down the street from the station and bought a drink. When I came out, I caught a glimpse of the same guy, standing partially turned away from me and partially behind the corner of a building across the street.

I had been trained to consider coincidences as

dangerous. So, rather than go straight to Jolene's, I started off in the other direction. I took the first corner and sped up, then took off at a sprint after rounding the next corner. There was a large bush in the yard of the second house, and I dived behind it.

My follower came around the corner and stopped. He looked around, turning his head in all directions, obviously baffled because he couldn't see me.

"What are you doing?" a woman's voice came from behind me. I looked up and saw a woman, probably in her sixties, with gray hair, glaring at me through her window screen.

"Shhhh. That man is stalking me," I whispered. "I think he's a rapist."

With a look of alarm, she slammed the window closed. I turned back, peeking through the bush, and saw my follower take off at a run down the street. As soon as he took the next corner, I went back around to the convenience store and used a pay phone to call Jolene.

"Hi. Do you know the little convenience store next to the train station near your house?"

"Yes?"

"Perhaps you could come and get me up there? I seem to have picked up a tail. I don't want to take him to your place."

"Thank you. I appreciate it. See you in about five minutes."

I waited inside the store, and when Jolene pulled in, I ran out and jumped in her car.

"The Brown Derby restaurant," I said. "Do you know where it is?"

"Yeah, why?"

"With any luck, that's where our Hunter is having breakfast."

The restaurant turned out to be on the north bank of the river, about two miles from the house where Hans Christian was staying. We pulled into the parking lot, and Jolene parked around the back.

She held out her palm holding a small plastic bag with the tracker she had prepared. "One side is sticky," she said. "*Very* sticky. If you touch it, we'll be tracking you." She turned the bag over. "This is the side you can touch. Stick it underneath one of the bumpers."

"He knows what I look like. Why don't you do it?"

Jolene pursed her mouth and seemed to be trying to think of something to refute my argument.

"You're probably right. But if I get caught, you have to bail me out."

"Not a problem."

We both got out of the car, and while she went looking for Christian's car, I snuck along the wall of the restaurant, trying to stay away from the windows. That required crawling under the windows on my hands and knees sometimes.

About the time I reached the front of the building, I saw Jolene walking back toward me.

"Come on. Let's go," she said as she walked past.

"Did you do it?"

"Yeah, it's all planted. Let's go see what we can see in the mirror."

I took a deep breath, looked around, then followed her, keeping my face turned away from the restaurant windows. I tried to slump a little, hoping to disguise the way I moved. I felt ridiculous.

Back in the car, Jolene pulled out the mirror and

showed it to me. A green dot, like a faint light, showed in the middle of the mirror with a red dot almost on top of it.

"The green dot is us," Jolene said. She pulled out another mirror that showed an identical pair of dots. "And this is the receiver for the tracker I planted in his glove. The glove is in his car."

That made some sense. I certainly wouldn't want to drive around wearing a Hunter's uniform. He probably kept it in the trunk of his car, along with his weapons, and changed somewhere after dark.

We waited for half an hour, then followed Christian when he came out of the restaurant. He drove along the north side of the river, crossed the east bridge, and then turned back toward town. His route took him by Rosie's, but he didn't stop. He did pull into my apartment complex, drive around all the buildings, then pulled back onto the street and continued toward downtown.

He parked in a parking garage next to city hall, then went to a movie theater, bought a ticket, and went in.

"What is he doing?" Jolene asked.

"Killing time until dark," I answered. "He's been here two months, and he's bored."

I considered that a good thing. It meant his edge might be dulled a little bit. I walked up to the ticket office and asked what time the movie was over,

Lizzy called Jolene, and they decided on a place to meet for lunch. With the trackers, there wasn't any reason for us to sit and wait on Christian. We would know when he began moving again.

We sat around and slowly drank a pitcher of beer until almost time for the movie to end, then walked back to the theater. Five minutes after we arrived, he came out.

We tracked him to a bar. And then we waited again, but not for long. Fifteen minutes after Christian entered the bar, Mietzner came down the street and also entered the bar.

"Well, I guess that solves the question about your spider," Jolene said.

After half an hour, Christian left. When it became obvious he was going to his car, Jolene went and got her car, then picked up Lizzy and me.

The sun was setting. Christian drove to a steakhouse and went inside. We went to a pizza place and had our dinner, then made it back to the steakhouse to find his car was still there.

Another hour of waiting.

"I don't think I'm cut out to be a cop or a private eye," Lizzy said. "This is booorrrring."

Christian finally came out and drove away. The tracking mirror lit up in the dark, and I was impressed with the elegance of the spell. We didn't have to keep the car we were following in sight, and I relaxed a little.

He drove across the river and turned to the right on a road following the river. Shortly thereafter, he took a left up into the foothills, but didn't go far, turning again into an upper-middle class neighborhood with nice homes on medium-sized lots.

"I've got a bad feeling about this," Jolene muttered as Christian took a couple more turns and then stopped.

"What's wrong?" I asked.

She didn't answer but pulled to a stop and killed the lights, her attention down the street to our left. I could see Christian's car with the lights out pulled to the curb.

The street was on the edge of the neighborhood, with forest to the north behind the houses.

"The third house from the corner is Frankie Jones's house," Jolene said. The house she indicated didn't have any lights on. Christian was parked several houses farther down the street.

We watched as he got out of his car, opened his trunk, then got back in his car. When he got out again, I could see that he'd changed clothes and was dressed all in black. He opened the trunk again, and in its light, I saw him pull a sword and some other things out. After closing the trunk, he walked toward us.

I opened my door. "Start the car, go back to where you can spot Frankie, and stop her when she comes home. Call her, and if you can't get hold of her, call Blair. We can trap him right here."

"Wait! Where are you going?" Lizzy asked.

"I'm just going to keep an eye on him. If Frankie gets by you and shows up, I'll try and help her. Now go!"

I walked up the sidewalk to the house in front of me, aware that the Hunter was watching us. Jolene started the car, pulled a U-turn, and drove away. I went around the side of the house and through a gate into the backyard, praying that the people who owned the house didn't have a dog.

Peeking over the fence, I saw the Hunter go past, not even looking in my direction, and disappearing into the forest that ran behind Frankie's house.

While I wasn't dressed in all-black like the Hunter was, I wore a navy coat and blue jeans, along with black boots. I took a black balaclava out of my pocket and pulled it over my head, covering my face.

The Hunter and I had received the same training,

but he was much older than I was, and my training was more recent. I had already noted several actions he had taken that bordered on sloppy. I attributed that to overconfidence and the lack of any recent challenge to his skill and expertise.

I figured that as long as I felt close to terrified at the notion of confronting him directly, overconfidence wouldn't be a problem. Other than sparring on the City's training grounds, I had never faced another Hunter, and had rarely even worked with one. For all I knew, my Masters had lied in praising my abilities. They had lied about everything else.

I waited for about ten minutes, fearful that the Hunter might be watching, then clambered over the fence into the next yard, then the next, until I was past where I'd last seen him. Crossing into the house's front yard and clinging to the shadows, I continued north, with houses behind me and forest across the street in front of me, until I reached the end of the street, where it dead-ended at the forest.

Circling around, I tried to spot the Hunter, knowing he was probably resting and perfectly still. Time stretched, and eventually, so did he, readjusting his position, then settling back. He was about thirty feet in front of me and twenty feet to my right in a place where he could see between Frankie's house and the one next door. He would know immediately if she pulled into her driveway.

It had been more than forty minutes since Jolene drove away. I had no idea of when Frankie would come home, or even if she would come home at all that night. Neither did the Hunter, unless Mietzner had given him some kind of inside information. When I was stalking a target, I had sometimes done a stakeout like that night after night, waiting for the perfect opening. Rarely was there an urgency factor. The Illuminati took the long view, and making sure of the kill without any suspicion was the paramount consideration.

## CHAPTER 26

Almost two hours after Jolene and Lizzy dropped me off at Frankie Jones's house, a car came down the street and pulled into the driveway. I heard the garage door open, and the Hunter moved from his position toward the house. The motor and clanking of the door opening smothered any noise that he made. I followed him.

I had strengthened my personal shield as much as I could and filled myself with power from the nearest ley line. I formed ley missiles in both of my hands.

The Hunter leapt over Frankie's fence and raced across the backyard, then hurdled the front fence. I followed him, but when I got to the front fence, I opened the gate and peered out. He stood in the light from the garage, sword in hand.

I pushed one of the ley missiles I held. He was unprepared for it—his shield flared, and he stumbled. Almost immediately, two fireballs came from the front of the house, dowsing him in flame. That was followed by a lightning bolt. Next, a mini-tornado enveloped him, and he staggered. I pushed the other energy ball I held and saw his shield flare again.

He whirled and ran directly toward me. I pulled on the ley line again and pushed the power at him. He bounced, just as if he'd run into a wall. Another fireball hit him from behind.

The Hunter stumbled backward, his head swiveling back and forth between me and his attackers in the front yard. I hit him with another ley missile, and I guess he made a decision, because he spun, raising his sword, and took off away from me at a run.

"Don't get in his way!" I screamed, chasing after him. "Move! Move!"

I saw Trevor standing in the middle of the street. He loosed a bolt of lightning at the Hunter, then dove out of the way as the black-clothed figure kept coming. I pushed another ley missile at the Hunter, and his shield flared again. I had the feeling that I could probably destroy the shield if I could hit him repeatedly, so I pushed another one at him. He broke to his left, and the ley missile missed, taking out a fire hydrant with spectacular results. A fountain erupted, bathing the street.

I chased after him, but he was at least six inches taller than I was, with longer legs. He headed toward the forest and disappeared into it. By the time I got there, I couldn't see anything, and I knew that to follow him farther would be suicide.

"Erin!" I heard Blair call from behind me. I turned and trudged toward him.

"He got away," I said. "I wasn't fast enough."

"Are you all right?" Blair raised his arms as though to draw me into a hug.

"Yeah, I'm fine," I said, ducking around him and admiring the fountain. A column of water shot forty feet in the air. I spotted Trevor and Josh, Frankie, and three or four of Blair's team. Jolene's car was parked down the street, with Lizzy and Jolene leaning against it.

Trevor walked over to me and bent close. Speaking softly, he said, "I could have tackled him. Why were you so freaked out? I was shielded."

"His sword is more than a sword," I said. "It's spelled. It's a magical artifact, and part of its magic is a nullification spell. It will cut right through all but the strongest shields. It will even cut through weak wards. That's why I didn't want to get close to him."

He gave me a shocked look, then said, "I see. Thanks."

Frankie approached, and I pointed at the Hunter's car. "That's his car. I'll bet you can lift prints from it. We also know where he's been staying. It's a house owned by Charles Mietzner. If you get a team up there in a hurry, he'll be stuck. Wearing his Hunter's garb and carrying that sword will make him a little conspicuous."

"Mietzner?" Frankie asked. "Oh, good Lord."

"If that's his handler, then we'd better stake out Mietzner's house as well," Blair said.

"You did a pretty good job of organizing that ambush," I said.

"Yeah, but he still got away," Blair said, watching the fountain. "Guess we should call the fire department."

---

From Frankie's, it was three miles to Mietzner's rental property and a little over seven miles to his new house.

The Hunter was on foot, and we assumed he would be traveling in such a way as to avoid notice.

It was decided that Frankie and some of Blair's team, along with a number of regular cops, would go to Mietzner's current residence and take him into 'protective custody.' After all, a homicidal maniac was loose, and as someone who had an association with Hans Christian, keeping Mietzner under wraps until everything worked itself out could be justified.

The rest of us headed to the rental house. The house was dark when we arrived, and Lizzy pointed out the booby traps. A team of cops took care of the physical traps and disposed of the explosives. Then Trevor and I set to work on the house's wards. While Trevor fired lightning bolt after lightning bolt at the house, I drew on the ley energy in the wards to create ley missiles and push them at the house.

It took about fifteen minutes, but we finally breached the wards. A SWAT team broke down the door and entered the house. Next, Lizzy was brought in to identify any magical traps, but she didn't find any. What we did find were maps with colored stick pins and notations identifying targets and kills.

The other contents of the house included his clothes and luggage, although it appeared he traveled light. That didn't surprise me. The refrigerator and cabinets were empty, which also didn't surprise me considering the credit card trail we found.

I approached Blair and said, "Have you given any thought to how you're going to capture him, and how you're going to hold him if you do?"

He gave me a rueful look. "That has been bothering me. We have cells that are warded and shackles that are spelled to prevent magic use, but after that display at Frankie's, capturing him might be a problem. Have you got any ideas?"

I took a deep breath. "Yeah. I'm not sure it will work, but I think it will. You'll have to pull all your people out. If he sniffs us, he'll back off, and the gods only know what he'll do next. My idea is to create a magical trap. I know that he can't breach wards I've set, because he tried at my apartment and failed. The house is too large to ward the whole thing, but I can ward one room, and set a trigger on the room's entrance. He trips the trigger and gets trapped in the room."

"That makes sense to me," Trevor said. "We hit him with everything but the kitchen sink at Frankie's, and it barely fazed him."

"We'll have to hurry, though," I said. "It's been an hour since he escaped, and he could be showing up any minute."

Blair gave orders and pulled all his people and the other cops back to hidden positions. All the cop cars were relocated out of sight of the roads leading in.

I walked into the house and decided the best room to use was the living room. There were multiple entrances to the house, but no matter how he came in, I figured he would go to the living room to peer out the front window.

I cast my wards at the room's four corners, then laid the trap trigger Sam had shown me at the front door and the entrance from the dining room. I didn't need anything personal of his as I only expected one guest. Backing out, I pulled energy from the ley line and fed it into the ward.

I snuck out through the garage and then out a side

door that led to the woods. Moving off around a hundred feet from the house, I found a fallen tree that created a sort of small cave and provided some shelter from the wind. Settling inside the hollow, I pulled my coat around me, set my personal shield, and pulled some ley magic to warm me a little.

Almost an hour later, when I began to wonder if the Hunter had already headed out of town, I heard a slight rustle of leaves. More soft sounds followed, and a few minutes later, I caught a tiny movement out of the corner of my eye. Focusing on that, I was able to make out the outline of a man about fifty feet from me, furtively moving closer to the house.

I never figured out what spooked him, but something did. He froze for a few minutes, then began working his way back up the hillside, away from the house.

Taking care to make less noise than my adversary, I also started away from the house, planning on circling around and trying to get ahead of him. He had to have crossed the road beyond the neighborhood, and there were cops stationed there. The fugitive had entered our ring, and if I could draw attention to him, we might still have a chance of capturing him.

Trying to maintain total quiet while aware of the need for speed, I made my way up the hill. The half-moon had risen, so I wasn't blundering around completely blind in the dark. My advantage was that I knew the Hunter was out there, and while he might suspect someone was stalking him, he couldn't be sure. I pulled as much ley power as I could hold, strengthening my shield, and also prepared to invoke the spell creating ley missiles. That magic had shown it affected his shield and had destroyed the ward he set on the house.

All my illusions of how stealthy I was being were destroyed when I reached the edge of a small clearing and found the Hunter waiting for me. He stood in the center of the clearing with his sword unsheathed. A balaclava covered his head except for his eyes, which were gray and cold.

I said the Word and pushed two ley missiles at him. His shield flared and shimmered, boosting my confidence.

Then a fireball swooshed toward me. I ducked it, and it exploded in the trees and brush, lighting them on fire.

"Real smart," I called, pushing two more ley missiles, causing him to stagger. "Light the forest on fire and burn both of us up."

He charged me, sword raised to cut me down. I waited until he was almost upon me, then dove forward, under his sword, and rolled past him. By the time he checked his charge and whirled around, I was back on my feet and pushed another ley missile at him. His shield visibly rippled.

"I thought you might have some honor," I said. "You plan to cut down an unarmed girl. Does that make you feel like a real man?"

He approached me slower, circling and trying to work me around so the fire was at my back. I hit him with another missile, and when he leaped toward me, I slammed him with ley energy, catching him in mid-leap and sending him back-flipping away from me.

As he crawled to his feet, I hit him with another missile.

"You want to be armed?" he asked, the first time I'd heard his voice. His left hand pulled his off-hand dagger

—half the length of his sword—from its sheath and flipped it at me. I had seen the trick on the practice fields many times and ducked, plucking the blade out of the air with my left hand as it flew over me.

He followed the blade spinning toward me, and I barely had time to block his blow as I straightened.

The dagger did even the odds a little, but the Hunter didn't give me the blade out of altruism. He hoped I would engage him in spite of his reach advantage and stop hitting him with the ley missiles. He was six inches taller than I was, and his blade was twice as long as mine.

I fended him off, but he pressed his advantage, backing me up and keeping my attention. I didn't dare take an instant to cast a spell, but my keeping the knife in my left hand bothered him. We were trained to use our blades with both hands, but I doubted the Hunter had fought many left-handed swordsmen, and my training was much more recent than his.

My quickness was negated by the length of his blade and his power. I missed one of his strikes, and though he didn't completely penetrate my shield, he weakened it. I was fighting a losing battle.

I dove to my right, rolling and coming up about seven feet from him. The burning trees were at my back, limiting my retreat options, but I had managed to gain some separation. We were both sweating and breathing heavily, and he hesitated before coming after me again.

With a Word, I invoked the Sword of Uriel, a spell my Masters said had been dead for six hundred years before I came along. A three-foot bar of green flame leaped from my right hand. I swung at the Hunter as he closed, but he jumped away.

"Scorpion." I saw his eyes widen in the sudden light that my magical blade created in the clearing.

"Fool," I returned. "Don't you know what the Illuminati are? You serve evil and corruption."

He laughed. "And you're a naïve little girl, for all your power. Throughout history, there have been rulers and subjects. The strong rule."

His little speech ended with him leaping at me, his sword raised for an overhead blow. I parried with my magical sword. Half of the Hunter's blade clanged against a rock ten feet away. He backed away, staring in shock at the stub of the sword he held in his hand.

I was as shocked as he was but recovered faster. I took two steps forward and drove my blade into his guts. He screamed, dropping his sword and grasping my blade with both hands. Then he screamed again, and as he pulled his hands away from the flaming blade, I saw his palms were blackened and smoking.

I pulled the sword out, and he dropped to his knees.

"You will die slowly and painfully," I said, "or I can end you painlessly. What is Mietzner's plan?"

He raised his head to look at my face, his ruined hands clasped around the wound in his belly. "Mietzner?" He looked puzzled. "Oh, the guy who owns the house. The politician."

The tone of his voice conveyed bewilderment. He truly didn't know Mietzner.

"Who is your contact?" I asked. "Hurry, or I'll leave you here to die in the flames."

The fire had spread quite a bit, and in the back of my mind I remembered the water-out-of-air trick Sam had pulled on that vampire. I had thought it was pretty neat when Sam did it, but it would have been even better with the forest on fire around us.

"Nava."

"Nava is Illuminati? Are there any more in Westport?"

"Yes, he is one of us. I don't know of any others."

Cursing myself for a fool, I granted him his release, driving the flaming blade into his chest. He stiffened, then his chin fell forward to his chest. When I pulled my sword out, he fell forward on his face. Not trusting him, I walked around him, placed the end of the sword at the base of his skull, and pushed, severing his spinal cord. Then I let the spell go. The only light in the clearing was from the burning fire.

The heat of the fire grew more intense, but I took the time to strip the Hunter of the sheath for his long knife, and also took the six shorter knives he carried. I had walked away from my own weapons, wanting never to wield them again. But obviously, violence had followed me. The long knife was a spelled blade, just as his sword was, but the shorter knives were not. I also took his Illuminati satellite phone and put it in my pocket along with his wallet.

And then I ran—away from my kill, away from the fire, away from my past once again. We had people holding Mietzner, but our most dangerous enemy was still on the loose.

## CHAPTER 27

Halfway down the hill, I heard a voice shout, "Halt! Stop right there and put your hands in the air!"

I was shielded, but I didn't want anyone realizing that bullets didn't harm me. Bad public relations. So, I did as he commanded. Two SWAT team members approached with assault rifles trained on me.

"Please tell Lieutenant Blair that Erin McLane is here, the Hunter is dead, and there's a forest fire burning on top of this hill."

They looked at each other, then one of them spoke into a little box he had clipped to his flak jacket. Then he listened, then he spoke again.

"It's okay," he called out. "She's with us. One of Blair's contractors."

I cautiously lowered my hands. They questioned me about the fire, then got on their radios again. Evidently the smoke could be seen from the road on the city side of the mountain, and I was told the fire department was on its way.

Making my way down the hill, I reached the house and found Blair.

"I got a call saying the Hunter is dead?"

"Yeah. He did tell me that Mietzner wasn't the one pulling his strings. He said it was Daniel Nava."

Blair stared at me, then got on the phone. He made one call, but I could tell no one answered. He dialed again and talked to someone for about five minutes. When he hung up, he called his team together, then talked to the head of the SWAT unit, and then to the lieutenant in charge of the normal cops.

Finally, he turned to me. "Nava showed up at Mietzner's with a few men, then he and Frankie took Mietzner away. They never showed up at the jail, and Frankie doesn't answer her phone. I sent some men to Nava's house."

"You might try Carleton House," I said.

His expression told me that he thought I'd lost my mind.

"Who were the men who showed up with Nava at Mietzner's?" I asked.

Blair shook his head. "I don't know. Captain Munroe didn't recognize them."

"Did they have very pale complexions? Nava has used Rodrick Barclay's thugs in the past, though he's also used mages."

He looked thoughtful. "Why would he take Frankie with him, though?"

Lizzy walked up, with Jolene, Trevor, and Josh trailing behind her.

"So that he can tell you that Jones and Mietzner killed each other," Lizzy said.

That got him moving.

"Did you See that?" I asked her in a low voice.

She was very pale, even more so than usual. "I'm Seeing all kinds of terrible things tonight. They can't all happen, because some of them are contradictory. Don't go with them. You don't have to." Her voice almost broke.

"Yeah, I do."

"Because Mietzner knows your secret."

"No, I don't think he does. But I'll never be safe here as long as he's alive. He'll bring in another Hunter." I was no longer worried about Mietzner. Nava was Illuminati, and I couldn't allow him to live.

She reached out and squeezed my arm. "Okay. We'll watch your back."

I looked over her head and saw the three mouseketeers nodding.

"You don't have to," I said.

Jolene shrugged. "It's what friends do. Besides, we know where he is."

Blair evidently heard that, because he spun around. "You do?"

Lizzy nodded. "He's not at Carleton House, but there's an old barn or something near there."

"The old carriage house," Jolene said. "Lizzy Saw it, and Trevor found an aerial view of the estate. My magic says that's where Nava's going. It feels right."

Blair called his team back together, then spoke with the SWAT captain again. A lot of people piled into cars and took off. Blair pulled me into the back seat of his car, along with Lizzy and Jolene. Detective Mackle, the orange-haired witch, rode up front with her boss.

When we got near the estate, Jolene directed Blair to drive past the paved road leading to Carleton

House. A hundred yards farther down the road, we came upon a narrow, dirt driveway almost hidden by the trees. A light rain had started to fall, and some mud and gravel had washed down onto the pavement, but we could still see recent car tracks on the driveway.

Blair killed his lights and drove on, pulling off the side of the road a hundred feet past the driveway. The dozen cars following us also doused their lights and found places to park.

The plan was to send the SWAT team ahead, take out any sentries, and surround the carriage house. Then the magic users would move in.

I pulled Blair aside. "You might want to send someone who can detect magic with your SWAT team," I told him. "I know Mietzner isn't a Hunter, but remember all those booby traps at the Hunter's place?"

"I don't really have anyone who can do that," he said.

I turned and motioned for Lizzy to come forward. "She can. I'll go to protect her."

While I explained what we needed to Lizzy, Blair had another talk with the SWAT captain. I felt bad, because I could see my friend was scared half to death, but she squared her shoulders and said she'd do it. I felt proud of her, and guilty, but I needed her Sight.

"Lizzy, I won't let anything happen to you. I'll have you covered all the way. Just stay behind me, okay?"

She nodded like a little girl, her eyes wide and her expression somber.

I threw up a shield over us to keep us dry and pulled her close to me. "Can you see? In the dark, I mean?" I asked her.

Lizzy chuckled and seemed to relax a bit. "Much better than you can."

I remembered she was half-Fae. I really didn't expect much in the way of traps or alarms, but better to be safe. Nava hadn't had time to prepare for his Hunter being exposed, and of course, he couldn't know the Hunter was dead.

We walked along the driveway, two SWAT team members flanking us and a little behind, their assault rifles at the ready. The carriage house came into view as we rounded a long curve. Beyond it were stables and a large open area with the main house in the distance to our right. Light showed dimly through a couple of the carriage house windows.

"I don't See any magic," Lizzy said. "There are people inside who are magical, though."

"Great. Thanks, Lizzy. You can go on back now. Tell Blair to send in the rest of the mages."

"Okay," she said, backing away from me. As she stepped out from under my shield, I noted that the rain didn't hit her. It wasn't as though she had her own shield deployed, but she just didn't get wet.

I signaled to the SWAT team guys. "No booby traps," I whispered.

They didn't look convinced, and I didn't blame them. No doubt they wondered what kind of madness afflicted the weird people they had to work with.

Soon, Trevor and Josh came up the drive with Blair.

"Any idea how many people are in there?" Blair asked.

"No. Do you want me to go look?" Without waiting for his response, I ran in a crouch to the building. Creeping along the wall, I reached one of the windows that showed light. I raised up and peeked in at the corner of the window. The first people I saw were vampires, two by the door to the room, and another one standing with his back to me. Mietzner and Nava stood in the middle of the room talking to each other.

Then I saw Frankie, her wrists and ankles shackled, with a gag in her mouth, lying against one wall. She was awake and glaring daggers at the two men.

I didn't think the Hunter had lied to me, but either Mietzner was also a member of the Illuminati, or he had been seduced by Nava's schemes. Another thought occurred to me as I made my way back to where Blair waited with my friends. The Hunter might not have known that Nava had a boss in the Order. Considering the amount of foreign trade that moved through Westport, the city was wealthy, and having two Illuminati stationed there would make sense. It wasn't even unusual that they knew each other, but it called into question a number of my assumptions. Were there any more members of the Order in the Columbia Club?

"Frankie's in there," I told Blair when I got back to him. "She doesn't appear to be hurt, but she's bound with those shackles you use for magic users. The problem is that both Nava and Mietzner are also there and acting like buddies. Do you know what their affinities are?"

"Nava's is fire," Josh said. "My dad knows him."

"Mietzner's is earth," Lizzy said. "And yes, Nava's is fire. I can See them."

"What does that mean?" Blair asked. "Earth?"

"Earthquakes," Trevor said. "He can open a hole under your feet, then cover you up."

Earth could do a lot more than that, but I didn't

think a dissertation on the subject was needed at that point. Getting buried alive was scary enough to make people wary.

"I also saw a bunch of vampires," I told them. "I suggest your SWAT guys load up on that incendiary ammunition you use."

"We have the building surrounded," Blair said. "Normally, we would call for the people inside to surrender."

"Normally, the crimes of the people inside are something you can take into court," I said. "If we don't get Frankie out alive, there aren't any witnesses. Nava and Mietzner will make up some story, and you won't have any way to disprove it. Vampires aren't witnesses. They're dead, remember?"

Looking over Blair's shoulder, I saw a man walking toward us from the direction of the stables. As he got closer, I recognized him as George Flynn, dressed in an elegant suit with a blood-red pocket square and tie.

"Lieutenant, Ms. McLane," Flynn said when he reached us. "You seem to be uncertain about how to proceed. Perhaps I can be of service."

Blair started to say something, but I cut him off. "Can you get all the vamps out of there?" I asked.

"Tsk, tsk. Such an ugly pejorative. Still, better than bloodsucker, but please, Ms. McLane, let us maintain some decorum."

I grinned at him. "I shall try and remember my manners, sir." I mocked a low curtsey, even though I wasn't wearing a dress.

"See that you do." He looked down his nose at me, but I could see the corners of his mouth twitch as he fought a smile.

"Please, dear sir, do you think you could persuade your clansmen to abandon the criminals inside yon domicile?" I asked, batting my eyes at him like a brainless idiot. I heard Jolene and Lizzy crack up, but I maintained my beseeching stare.

Flynn's smile broke free. "Anything for such a charming lady."

He turned and marched along the road to the carriage house, pulled open a door, and disappeared inside.

"And why would he help us?" Blair asked.

"Brownie points. Good will and the chance to twist Rodrick Barclay's tail."

Almost immediately, a couple of vampires exited the building and started across the field toward the main house. Over the next few minutes, a dozen more followed, and finally, Flynn himself came out.

"Only three people left inside," Flynn said. "A couple of them were a bit concerned that Barclay ordered his people to leave, but I don't think they suspect why. Let me know if I can do you any further service."

He bowed, and I curtseyed again, then he wandered off into the dark.

## CHAPTER 28

"Well, that simplifies things," Blair said. "Any suggestions as to what we do next?"

"I think you have very few choices," I said. "You can invite them to come out and hope they don't kill Frankie. You can give them a head start and not pursue them if they let her go. You can light the place on fire and hope we can rescue her in time, or you can assault every door, and hope it distracts them enough that I can rescue her during the confusion."

"And why should you be the one to rescue her?"

"Because my shields are stronger than anyone else's. But I'm not hung up on it. If someone else is better qualified, I'll gladly sit out here where it's safe."

Detective Mackle pulled at his sleeve. "She has a point, Boss."

"You do need to make up your mind soon, though," Lizzy said. "They didn't bring her out here for a romantic tryst." I shot Lizzy a glance and could clearly see she was very agitated. I wished for a moment I could see what she was Seeing, then decided I was better off without knowing.

We counted six doors into the carriage house, including the large double doors at each end that the horses and carriages had used when Lord Carleton built the place. Blair stationed two mages at each of the small doors, backed up by two SWAT men. Detective Mackle set wards blocking the two large double doors.

I positioned myself by the door closest to the room where the men had Frankie. It seemed like I stood there forever before the signal finally came. A single gunshot.

A SWAT man had a battering ram to break down the door, but I didn't wait for him. I pushed ley energy at the door, and it exploded inward. I reinforced my shield for about the sixth time and dashed through the door.

I was in a small room with one door on the right at the other end. Before I could move forward, Daniel Nava stepped into the room, a pistol leveled at me.

"You stupid, interfering bitch," he whined.

"Me? I was perfectly happy just living my life until you started sending your goons to attack me."

He turned red in the face, his eyes narrowed, and he tensed—all signs someone is preparing to pull the trigger. In spite of my shield, my training and instincts had me moving before he fired the shot.

Out of the corner of my eye, I saw a flash of something pink and white, but I was already charging Nava. He got off two more shots before I ran into him, my shield absorbing the energy of his shield. His eyes bulged as my hand closed on his throat, and his head hit the wall with a sound like a bat hitting a baseball.

I spun through the doorway into the next room.

Mietzner stood in the middle of the room, and he didn't look happy. Frankie still lay on the floor where I had seen her earlier, and she was still alive.

"You never did call me," Mietzner said. "All that flirting. I had hoped to avoid this kind of scene."

"Sorry to disappoint you," I said, pushing a ley missile at him. It flared when it hit his shield. I didn't want him talking. The less Frankie knew about the situation and Mietzner and me, the better.

A deep rumbling sound was accompanied by the world lurching and the floorboards groaning and squeaking in protest. I pushed another ley missile at him and followed it with a push of ley energy. His shield flared again, but not as brightly, and he staggered.

The floor rolled as though we were on a ship. The outside stone wall of the room crumpled, and Mietzner started to turn in that direction, preparing to run.

My next ley missile destroyed his shield, and the following one vaporized him, just as it had the vampires at the flour mill. The earthquake calmed down, the tremors diminishing in strength. I rushed across the room, grabbed the chain between the shackles on Frankie's wrists, and dragged her outside amidst a rain of falling debris. I got her far enough away from the building that she wouldn't be hit with any more debris if it fell down.

I looked around, searching in particular for one person. She wasn't anywhere to be seen, so I ran back toward the building.

Lizzy lay on the floor of the room where I'd left Nava, her head in Trevor's lap. She was covered in blood and clutched her stomach. I knew immediately what had happened. She Saw Nava shoot me and jumped between us to try and prevent it.

"Oh, Lizzy," I said, kneeling down beside her. I pried her hands away from her abdomen and ripped her dress open. The bullet had entered just below her ribs on her right side and exited her back. There was an awful lot of blood.

"Call an ambulance," Blair shouted. "Get a doctor."

"Why, Lizzy? I was shielded, silly girl. I told you to stay behind me."

"It hurts, Erin," she said, tears rolling down her cheeks. "It hurts so damned bad."

I stood and walked over to Nava, who was unconscious on the floor. Grabbing him by the hair, I dragged him over to where Lizzy lay. I shoved one hand inside his shirt and put my other hand over Lizzy's heart. Then I began pulling his life's energy out of him and feeding it into her.

"She doesn't need a doctor, Trevor," I said. "She needs a healer, and she needs one fast. We're going to lose her." I felt tears roll down my own cheeks. I could feel her pain, but I had my own pain, too. She was my friend, and I felt as though Nava had reached inside me and ripped something precious out of me.

Trevor reached for Lizzy's purse, pulled out her phone, and punched a couple of buttons.

"Lizzy's hurt very badly," he said into the phone. "She needs you now." He listened for a moment, then said, "The carriage house at Carleton House."

He put the phone down, and shot a glance at Nava, who was visibly shriveling, then looked at Lizzy's face. He gave me a nod of approval.

Five minutes later, a woman walked in. Several

inches short of five feet, with thick pink hair past her waist, she had large, sharply slanted eyes with slit pupils, sharp cheekbones, a heart-shaped mouth and a pointed chin. She was beautiful, but no one who saw her could possibly think she was human.

She knelt down on Lizzy's other side and put her hand on Lizzy's head, then her other hand slid next to mine on Lizzy's chest. The Fae woman raised her eyes to meet mine, and then I felt a jolt of magic of a flavor that was completely alien.

The bleeding stopped, and Lizzy slipped into what seemed like a restful sleep. The Fae woman picked Lizzy up and rose to her feet. She carried the girl outside, then turned back to me. In a voice that sounded like silver bells, she said, "You saved my daughter's life. I will not forget."

The two women sank into the earth, leaving no trace of where they had gone.

---

I felt someone come through the door into the bar and turned to see who it was. Frankie Jones slid onto a barstool and smiled at me.

"And what can I do for our Acting District Attorney?" I asked.

"A cosmo."

"Coming right up."

I mixed her drink and took it to her. She pushed a twenty across the bar and said, "Thanks, Erin. Thanks for saving my life."

I winked at her and said, "No problem. I mean, if

you can't depend on your friendly neighborhood bartender, who can you depend on?"

When I took her change to her, I asked, "Any luck on your investigation into the Columbia Club?"

"Some. My father has been a big help. So far, we haven't turned up any evidence of the Illuminati, except for what we found at Nava's and Mietzner's houses. And even that wasn't much."

I hadn't expected she would find very much. The Illuminati hadn't stayed hidden for centuries by leaving evidence of their existence lying around. Everything I knew about them I carried in my head, except for the contents of a book no one had ever planned for me to read.

"They both had satellite phones, and we can't figure out who manufactured them," Frankie said, "but they don't connect to anything."

We chatted a while longer, then she said she was going to try and get a good night's sleep and left. I watched her go, hoping that my life would have a chance of getting on some kind of normal track now that the threat of the Illuminati looked like it was over.

I had hidden the Hunter's satellite phone with the book, just in case I might ever need it. But when I asked Trevor about the Illuminati's website, he shook his head.

"I tried to check on it, just out of curiosity," he said. "It throws a four-oh-four error."

"What's that?" I asked.

"Page not found. I tried to ping their server, and it's gone. Not even any old artifacts. Looks like they completely turned everything off and disconnected it."

"Or maybe they weren't paranoid," I said.

He gave me a strange look. "How so?"

"Well, they were a conspiracy group, right? Maybe someone bombed them."

He laughed and then we went out and got a pizza.

---

If you enjoyed **Shadow Hunter** I hope you will take a few moments to leave a brief review on the site where you purchased your copy. It helps to share your experience with other readers. Potential readers depend on comments from people like you to help guide their purchasing decisions. Thank you for your time!

***Get updates on new book releases, promotions, contests and giveaways! Sign up for my newsletter.***

BOOKS BY BR KINGSOLVER ·

The Dark Streets Series

***Gods and Demons***

***Dragon's Egg***

***Witches' Brew***

The Chameleon Assassin Series

***Chameleon Assassin***

***Chameleon Uncovered***

***Chameleon's Challenge***

***Chameleon's Death Dance***

***Diamonds and Blood***

The Telepathic Clans Saga

***The Succubus Gift***

***Succubus Unleashed***

***Broken Dolls***

***Succubus Rising***

***Succubus Ascendant***

Other books

***I'll Sing for my Dinner***

***Trust***

Short Stories in Anthologies

*Here, Kitty Kitty*

*Bellator*

## WHERE TO FIND ME ONLINE

BRKingsolver.com
Facebook
Twitter

Printed in Great Britain
by Amazon